THE SENECA WORLD OF GA-NO-SAY-YEH

(Peter Crouse, White Captive)

Joseph A. Francello, Ph.D.
Muhlenberg College

UNIVERSITY PRESS OF AMERICA

LANHAM • NEW YORK • LONDON

University Press of America,™ Inc.

4720 Boston Way
Lanham, MD 20706

3 Henrietta Street
London WC2E 8LU England

Printed in the United States of America

ISBN: 0-8191-1141-4

Library of Congress Number: 80-1358

TO

THE MEMORY OF

LEO C. COOPER

HA-YEN-DO-NEES (THE WOODMAKER)

HERON CLAN

OF THE

SENECA NATION

A FINER FRIEND ONE COULD NOT FIND
AMONG ANY PEOPLE ON THIS EARTH

LEO COOPER AT PETER CROUSE GRAVE SITE

PETER CROUSE-DIEDJUNE 27, 1847

AGED 86 YEARS

LEO, A RETIRED STEEL-RIGGER, HEADED BURIAL RELOCATION AND PLACED CAPTIVE IN NEW GRAVE. A PAST-PRESIDENT OF THE SENECA NATION,LEO WAS A VALUABLE FRIEND AND AIDE OF THE AUTHOR.

ENJOYING A NICE DAY AT THE ALLEGANY RESERVATION WERE, LEFT TO RIGHT, BOB CROUSE (DIRECT DESCENDANT OF PETER CROUSE), MERLE DEARDORFF (LONGTIME FRIEND AND ETHNOGRAPHER OF THE SENECAS), AND CHESTER RED-EYE (WELL-KNOWN SENECA INDIAN).
COURTESY OF STRATTON PHOTO, WARREN CO. HISTORICAL SOCIETY, PENNSYLVANIA.

FOLLOWERS OF HANDSOME LAKE - ED CURRY (WITH CANE) AND HARRY WATT VISIT OUTSIDE THE LONGHOUSE AT STEAMBURG. ED HAD JUST PREACHED THE CODE AND HARRY IS A HIGHLY RESPECTED LEADER ON THE RESERVATION.

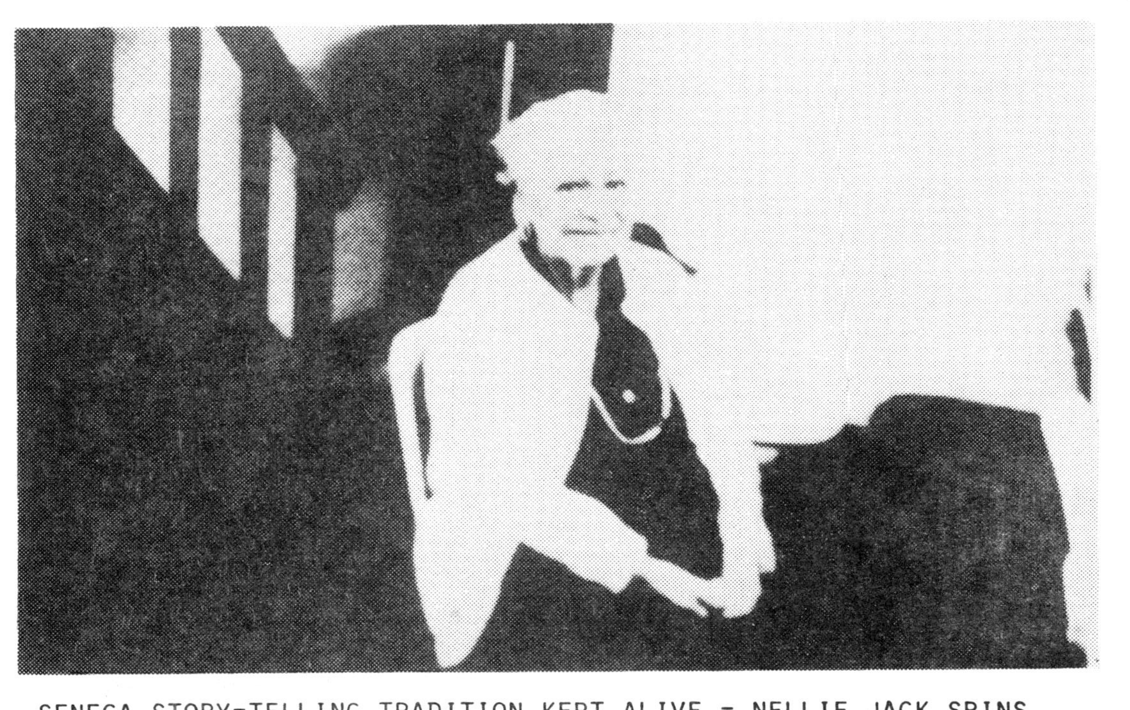

SENECA STORY-TELLING TRADITION KEPT ALIVE - NELLIE JACK SPINS A GOOD ONE FOR VISITING MUHLENBERG COLLEGE STUDENTS. NELLIE MADE UP THE STORY RIGHT THEN AND THERE FOR A HIGHLY APPRECIATIVE AUDIENCE.

DEMA CROUSE STOFFER, DESCENDANT OF PETER CROUSE, PAUSES FOR A MOMENT DURING CHURCH SOCIAL. SHE WAS VERY HELPFUL TO THE AUTHOR AND SHOWED HIM A HIGHLY-TREASURED COPY OF THE PROGRAM FOR THE CROUSE FAMILY REUNION OF 1911.

GEORGE HERON, DESCENDANT OF PETER CROUSE, OUTSTANDING ATHLETE, PAST-PRESIDENT OF THE SENECA NATION, PICTURED OUTSIDE THE PRESBYTERIAN CHURCH WHERE HE SERVES AS AN ELDER. ABOUT TO RETIRE FROM HIGH STEEL, HE PLANS COLLEGE LECTURE CIRCUIT.

DOROTHY JIMERSON, CLAN MOTHER OF HERON CLAN, WAS VERY PROUD TO BE PHOTOGRAPHED IN AUTHENTIC SENECA WOMAN'S DRESS MADE ENTIRELY BY HER. SHE HAD APPEARED ON A BUFFALO, NEW YORK, TV SHOW SHORTLY BEFORE THIS PICTURE WAS TAKEN.

TABLE OF CONTENTS

CHAPTER 1

TURMOIL OF THE WESTERN FRONTIER

Probably no one in the field heard anything to cause alarm. The war party of Indians closing in for the attack moved quietly and carefully so as to take by surprise the three working there. Moccasin-covered feet stepped lightly. No twig was snapped or leaves disturbed to give warning. The forest nearby continued its usual sounds of an early spring day in western Pennsylvania so that its copper-colored children could conclude their deadly play.

Suddenly there came the dreaded war whoop with its fierce challenge to white invasion. Paint-smeared warriors leaped to the attack, tomahawks and knives flashing, and in a few moments it was over.

The man and his older son were killed and scalped but the life of the younger boy was spared. It cannot really be ascertained why at such a time a life was spared. Perhaps the youthfulness of the younger boy struck a responsive chord in the mind of his attacker, who may have had a son the same age in a smoky, bark-covered cabin in the wilderness of the upper Allegheny. Or possibly the warrior was anticipating the pleasure of parading a live captive through his home village. We can never be certain except that something prompted the Indian to forego the four dollars he could have received from the British agent at Fort Niagara on the existing practice of eight dollars for a white male adult, six dollars for a white female adult, four dollars for an adolescent white and two dollars for a white infant's scalp. The so-called savage red man did not, in this case, succumb to the blandishments of the so-called civilized white man. The boy, whose name was Peter Crouse, thus became one of that unique group in American Colonial history known as "white captives."

The date was April 15, 1778, and the western frontier was once again ablaze--Fort Pitt was on the defensive with smaller strongholds such as Fort Martin[1] subject to strong Indian pressure. Some settlers had ventured back to their fields that early spring day and this had set the scene for the killing of Peter Crouse's father and brother along Dunkard's Creek, a tributary of the Monongahela River. One more "border incident" had taken place.

Thomas Boyd, a biographer of the dreaded renegade, Simon Girty, characterizes the frontier at this time as a region of great destruction and conflict.

> American pioneers who crossed over the Alleghanies and settled westward of Pittsburgh during the last quarter of the eighteenth century went into a wilderness where the forces of destruction flourished . . .for thirty years musketball and speeding arrowhead crossed and recrossed over clearing and occasional plain . . . cornfields trampled and charred . . . Scalps were ripped by Indian and white man alike. Mercy was a word not greatly honored by anyone.[2]

The area around the Great Lakes, western New York State, western Pennsylvania, and the upper Ohio was bathed in bloody violence from early times. Before the coming of the white man, aboriginal peoples had struggled for mastery, with the Iroquois federation achieving polical hegemony by the middle of the seventeenth century. Later, French and English interests collided, bringing bloody encounters of the so-called French and Indian War of the mid-eighteenth century. With this hardly over, came the American Colonial struggle against England and more bloodshed.

"Border incidents" is the term often used to refer to specific acts of violence and terror that took place almost continuously on this western frontier.

Frederick Jackson Turner's evaluation of the frontier as "the meeting point between savagery and civilization" is misleading in that it implies savagery on the part of the Indians and civilization on the part of the whites. In looking at the border incidents, it seems more accurate to say that savagery existed on both sides.

In the spring of 1774, four years before the capture of Peter Crouse, a series of hostilities known as "Lord Dunmore's War" exploded the uneasy relations between white and red man on the western frontier. It began with several Indians murdered by whites who attempted to justify their behavior with very doubtful reasons. The entire family of an Indian named Logan was murdered even though he had been a staunch friend and had refused to take the warpath against the whites. This incident turned Logan into a formidable foe of the settlers.

When peace was finally declared, Logan had survived but was an embittered and lonely man. He refused to attend any of the parleys but he sent a message which became famous for its anguish, sincerity, and directness.

> I appeal to any white to say if ever he entered Logan's cabin hungry, and he gave him not meat; if ever he came cold and naked and he clothed him not . . .
>
> I had even thought to have lived with you but for the injuries of one man, Colonel Cresap, the last spring, in cold blood, and unprovoked, murdered all the relations of Logan, not even sparing my women and children.
>
> There runs not a drop of my blood in the veins of any living creature . . . Who is there to mourn for Logan? -- Not one![3]

Later, Logan himself was murdered by whites and the extinction of his family was completed.

The Indians struck back with all the fury of a powerful people who knew they were facing loss of their lands, destruction of their way of life, and exile to the west, or life on a reservation for the survivors. We see the result of some of the Indian handiwork in the journal of Colonel Charles Lewis of Fredericksburg, Virginia. In an entry dated December 6, 1755, he states:

> . . .I saw the most horrid, shocking sight I ever yet beheld. At a house adjoining the cornfield in which our soldiers were employed in gathering corn, we saw the bodies of three different people, who were first massacred, then scalped, and afterwards thrown into the fire; these bodies were not yet quite consumed, with the flesh of many parts of them. We saw the clothes of these people yet bloody, and the stakes or clubs, the instruments of their death, still bloody and their brains sticking on them.[4]

The prevailing attitude of the whites toward the Indian was definitely that of superiority, seeing themselves as "civilized" people having to contend with the unfeeling savage. William Walton in commenting on the captivity of Benjamin Gilbert, who like Peter Crouse, was taken from his farm on the Pennsylvania frontier, stated that the Indians "from infancy are taught a hardness of heart which deprives them of the common feelings of humanity."[5] He also went on to say that "when we compare the temper and customs of these people with those of our own colour, how much cause have we to be thankful for the superiority we derive from the blessings of civilization.[6]

It is shocking to note that white antagonism toward the Indian was not only a general feeling on the part of the American population but was also reflected in the viewpoint of a number of the clergy. A protest against this kind of feeling was voiced by the Quaker Robert Smith, editor of the publication The Friend:

> . . . a murderous, fanatical spirit had been spread amongst certain inhabitants of Pennsylvania which would have doomed all the Indians to destruction. It was openly declared and that by persons professing to be ministers of the gospel, that the heathens ought not to be permitted to live in the land. That this country had been given to the white settlers, and that as Joshua and the children of Israel were to destroy the Cannaanites, so it was their duty to kill all the Indians.[7]

Fortunately for Peter Crouse and other white captives like him, the Seneca Indians did not see it as their duty to kill all whites. Their traditions allowed greater selectivity than a blanket sanction against every living enemy. It seemed more likely to the Indian that the whites would soon annihilate each other. Scarcely had the moans and groans of the wounded and dying of the French and Indian War subsided when a new conflict pitting whites against each other broke out.

The outbreak of the American Revolution was rather incomprehensible to the red man. He had been able to fathom the French versus English struggle when it was explained as a violent difference of opinion between the followers of one great father, the English king, and the followers of another great father, the French king. That the followers of the English king should now be fighting other followers of the English king was too much of a contradiction in the minds of a people who were politically sophisticated enough to have enjoyed a federation of five nations for several centuries.

Seneca raiding of the kind which took young Peter Crouse was by no means an indication of decisiveness toward the colonial war against England. The Great Council of the Iroquois federation had not been able to agree, with some sachems in favor of continuing as allies of the English while others favored entering on the side of the American colonists. The resulting political fragmentation, with no official decision, left participation a local matter. Due to the nature of the frontier settlement with its poor communication and isolation, the American colonists became targets of opportunity for ambitious Indian war captains, anxious to establish reputations as fearsome fighting men. There were always adventurous young braves willing to follow these chiefs and the British agents were effective in stirring them up with gifts of guns, whiskey, and payments for scalps.

It is also true that some adventurous whites saw the opening of hostilities as a chance for personal gain. In the same manner that the Indians understood the vulnerability of the white settlers, the white opportunists clearly understood the Indian weaknesses which left them open to exploitation. British agents were not entirely to blame for Indian depredation.

> . . .The best and the worst of the race gather upon the borders of civilization. As usual, there were those not averse to an Indian war for the sake of the spoils and the excitement. To keep faith with the Indians, on the part of the authorities, proved often exceedingly difficult . . . The horrors of Indian warfare were not entirely due to British incitement. In many cases, American frontiersmen but reaped the bitter harvest of their own rash deeds.[8]

Barely one year after the capture of Peter Crouse, the American colonists decided to break the military power of the Iroquois by armed invasion. General Washington ordered a two-pronged attack against the league in 1779. One led by General Sullivan from the east against the Indian villages near Elmira and Rochester, and the other led by General Brodhead stiking north from Fort Pitt against the Indian villages on the upper Allegheny.

Peter Crouse was directly affected by Brodhead's campaign as it reched the village where Peter was living. General Brodhead reported his troops burned houses and destroyed corn crops for three days. When his soldiers reached Jenuchsadaga, Cornplanter's village, the Indians fled across the river and watched from a nearby mountaintop. It must have been with mixed feelings that Peter Crouse saw white soldiers burning and destroying the village that had sheltered him as one of its own. After Brodhead withdrew, the village was rebuilt and the Indians dug up caches of corn which had been hidden to see them through this kind of emergency.

The disruption of Indian affairs caused by the American Revolution is eloquently stated in a letter sent by the Senecas to the State of New York November 21, 1798. The sachems, chiefs, and warriors of the Seneca Nation stated:

> . . . Brothers - you will recollect the late contest between you and your father the great King of England. This contest threw the inhabitants of this whole land into a great tumult and commotion, like a raging whirlwind which tears up the trees, and tosses to and fro, the leaves so that no one knows from whence they come or where they will fall.[9]

The American Revolution and series of events connected with it became a watershed for the Iroquois. Their power and military control of territory was broken forever. Only a shadow of their former selves remained. In addition to the humility of defeat and loss of territory, one of the provisions of the peace treaty with the United States required the surrender of all white captives taken by the Indians.

Peter Crouse should have been able to return to white society in 1784 as in that year at the Treaty of Fort Stanwix a treaty of friendship was concluded by Iroquois representatives and the U.S Government. Boundaries were redefined, with tremendous loss of territory for the Indians and the Six Nations agreed to surrender all their captives.[10] Peter, however, did not choose to return.

It surprised many Americans to find that some captives did not wish to return to white society and that the Indians were very reluctant to give them up. Very few people in the United States realized the deep attachments which adoption had brought about for both the Indian and the white captives.

The highly respected Seneca, "Farmer's Brother" in an emotional speech given during a council of the Six Nations at Genesee River in 1798, referred to white children taken captive:

> We adopted them into our families, and made them our children. We nourished them and loved them . . They lived with us many years. At length the Great Spirit spoke to the whirlwind . . . The path of peace was opened . . . these adopted children left us to seek their relations. We wished them to return among us, and promised, if they would return and live in our country, to give each of them a seat of land for them and their children to sit down upon.[11]

The children of Peter Crouse and their children's children, and descendants of his to present day have had their "seat of land" on the Allegany Reservation. Peter made his decision to stay with his adopted people and voluntarily lived out a long life at the place he had first been brought to as a terrified captive lad.

FOOTNOTES

CHAPTER I

[1]A small fort commanded by Major Martin, and located on a tributary of the Monongahela River.

[2]Thomas Boyd, Simon Girty the White Savage (New York: Minton, Balch and Co., 1928), p. 3.

[3]Samuel G. Drake, Indian Biography (Boston: Josiah Drake, 1832), pp.164-164.

[4]Lyman C. Draper, Manuscripts (Madison: State Historical Society of Wisconsin) Vol. 21, p. 51.

[5]William Walton, A Narrative of the Captivity of Benjamin Gilbert (Philadelphia: Cruckshank, 1784), p. iv.

[6]Ibid., p. 16.

[7]The Friend (Philadelphia: Joseph Mite and Co., 1845), Vol. XVIII, p. 63.

[8]Reuben Gold Thwaites and Louise Phillips Kellogg, The Revolution on the Upper Ohio (Madison, Wisc.: Wisconsin Historical Society, 1908), p. xviii.

[9]Henry O'Reilly, Papers Pertaining to the Six Nations (New York Historical Society microfilmed 1948), Vol. 13.

[10]O. Turner, Pioneer History of the Holland Purchase, (Buffalo: Jewett, Thomas & Co., 1849), p. 304.

[11]Ibid., p. 291.

CHAPTER 2

PETER, AS A CAPTIVE

Peter Crouse had no choice but to accompany the men who had so suddenly burst upon his life, becoming his family's murderers and his benefactors at the same time. It is doubtful he had very much time to reflect on the tragedy and irony of the situation. The usual pattern followed by Indians holding a captive was a series of forced marches, with no stopping for food or fire, until a good distance away from the scene of depredation.

During the period of hard flight, captives were brutally forced onward with blows and threats of death. Should the Indians become convinced they were being endangered by a slow captive, a fatal blow with the tomahawk was swiftly administered to the laggard.

The young captive passed this first critical test at the hands of his captors. There have been conflicting accounts as to his age at the time. William Adams in his History of Cattaraugus County takes note of Peter Crouse as a German who was captured by Indians on the Monongahela when seven years old and adopted into their tribe.[1]

A more plausible figure is given by the Reverend Timoth Alden, President of Allegheny College, who made several trips as a Christian missionary to the Allegheny Reservation early in the nineteenth century. While staying at the Crouse cabin on one of these visits, he was told by Peter that he was fourteen years old at the time of his capture.[2]

The party of Indians who captured him may have been a mixture of Senecas, Delawares. Mingoes, and even some white renegades, possibly including the notorious Simon Girty. Although no actual documentation is available, a number of accounts place Girty in the raiding party.

Both time and place make it quite possible Girty was involved in the Crouse capture. Simon Girty slipped away from Fort Pitt the night of March 28, 1778, and was with marauding Indians from the spring of 1778 onward.[14]

A military report from Colonel Evans to General Hand, dated April 18, 1778, tells of an attack by Indians on the fifteenth of that month in the area around a tributary of the Monongahela, close to the Virginia border. The colonel goes on to say that three men, James Stuart, James Smalley, and Peter Crouse were killed and that among the prisoners taken by the Indians were sons of the three men killed.[4] This military source would set the actual date of capture as April 15, 1778. If Girty left Fort Pitt in March of that year, it is quite possible he dallied in the area for several weeks.

The place, Dunkard's Creek, was a likely area for Girty to be lurking as an Indian war trail followed the creek for a distance, making that area "especially exposed to depredations."[5]

The surveyor, Samuel Maclay, made one of the earliest references to Peter Crouse as an Indian when he noted in his journal of 1790: "Monday, July 5, . . we saw a Dutchman who in the war had been taken prisoner and it seem(s) chused to continue with the Indians."[6]

When the historian Lyman C. Draper, made his tour of western New York and Pennsylvania in 1850 his main interpreter was the son of Peter Crouse, also named Peter. Peter told Draper that his father was captured by Senecas in 1777 and all his father's family killed except one brother who was away at the time and who later settled in Alabama.

According to the account given to Draper,

Peter Crouse was sixteen years old when captured and died in 1847 at the age of 86 years.[7] Whatever the discrepancies, there is no doubt Peter received an exposure to Seneca war customs at an early age.

Seneca war customs were in line with the Iroquois concept of the proper maintenance of peace. The legend of Hiawatha and Deganawidah stressed the goal of the confederacy as that of peaceful relations within the group of five nations. The council fire was to replace the tomahawk for the settling of differences within but the attitude toward outsiders was an aggressive policy of war and domination.

A red-painted tomahawk, decorated with red feathers and a piece of black wampum, was driven deep into the village war post to signify that warrior chiefs could organize raids against the designated enemy. A chief who wished to lead a war party attracted volunteers by giving a succession of fierce war whoops, then going up to the post and striking it with his own tomahawk. After this, he began a war dance. Those who wished to go with him signified their intention by going up to the post, striking it with their own tomahawks and then joining the group dancing the war dance. The women of the village made their contribution by preparing the rations the men would carry while on the war path.[8]

The war party that took Peter Crouse prisoner was not, however, a disciplined body of soldiers under command of a superior officer. Each warrior was still his own man, having voluntarily put himself under the leadership of the war chief but reserving to himself the option of breaking off the relationship any time he felt there was sufficient reason to do so.

The traditions of the warpath called for teamwork and cooperation but it was always among equals.

> . . .war making was not a subject for discipline. Neither the civil chiefs nor the councils had any final authority on this point . . . The records show, not the warrior's refusal to obey, but the official lack of legal power to command. Obedience was by the braves' consent.[9]

Returning war parties were extremely proud of their prisoners, each one "belonging" to the warrior who had taken him or her. Before entering the village, the raiding party gave a series of calls announcing its imminent arrival. This generated great excitement in the village and assured the braves of a large audience for the triumphal re-entry. War paint was put on afresh from supplies that had been hidden a short distance from the village and all was made ready so they could play the part of returning heroes.

Adult male captives were generally given a rough reception by the assembled villagers. The usual greeting was shouts of derision and waving of clubs, sticks, and fists. Two lines were formed and the prisoner was told he should try to reach a certain goal. There is no record that Peter Crouse was required to undergo any kind of ordeal upon reaching the Indian village that was to be his new home. In the case of Horatio Jones taken as an adult male, it was a different story.

Jones was captured by Senecas in 1781 and though his life with the Indians afterwards was quite pleasant, his introduction to their customs took the form of a rough initiation.

> . . .When the lines were formed between which the prisoners were to pass, Jack Berry (a Seneca friend) took Jones to the head of the lines and pointed to him the goal at which if he arrived in safety he was free. As he approached he

> observed that the occupants stood with uplifted weapons on each side, and when the word was given to start, Jones chose a close connection to one side . . . i.e., run so close that they had no room to swing their arms and he got through . . . into his future home and was met by his adopted mother.[10]

Fortunately for Peter Crouse, there was a strong tradition in the war customs of the Seneca that they did not make war on women and children. Captives who were young, and female captives, were not subjected to torture or to ordeals such as running the gauntlet. Great sensitivity was shown by the Senecas to any implication they mistreated women or children taken in battle.

The land surveyor, John Adlum, was severely rebuked by Chief Cornplanter when Adlum suggested that if there should be another war the Indians should be better behaved and "cease to put to death women and children."

> . . .These words were scarcely uttered before every man present, simultaneously rose on his feet, and all fixed their eyes on me with a mixture of Sternness and resentment . . . (Cornplanter) spoke loud and with great emphasis and energy - By saying Who began that business . . .if we were successful (in battle) we took the women and children prisoners whom we invariably adopted into our families. . .[11]

The tradition of adoption, referred to by Chief Cornplanter in his rebuttal to the charge that the Senecas made war on women and children, has been important in the Seneca value system for many centuries. It is a custom which has a practical side, an emotional dimension, and one which is ingeniously integrated within the political and kinship system of clan, tribe, and confederacy.

The practical aspect can be seen in that adoption enabled the Seneca to replace men who were lost in battle or died of old age and disease. By today's standards, the number of warriors that could be put into the field was modest and families were small.

> Adoption . . . was in a large measure responsible for the dominance of the Iroquois, so far as it raised their manpower above the normal rate of increase by births and cushioned the effect of mortalities. It was adoption which kept the Iroquois armies staffed.[12]

The Seneca author, Arthur C Parker, stresses the importance of adoption as a means of maintaining population level. Parker states that the wars engaged in by the Iroquois in the seventeenth century, 1630-1675, "had reduced the Iroquois by nearly one-half, and yet by their policy of adoption and naturalization they had an even greater population in their towns than when they began their bloody onslaughts."[13]

That adoption carried with it very strong emotional feelings can be seen in various accounts of Iroquois behavior in that situation. The new parent or parents became protective and showed affection and tenderness such as they would to a family member returning after a long absence. If possible, they attempted to meet them some distance from the village and take them to their new home by a different route than that of the returning war party.[14] This enabled the prisoner to avoid the ugly confrontation at the village limits and demonstrated the concern and sincerity of his new parents. The other villagers knew this took place but did not attempt to interfere as it was something a family was fully expected to do for one of its members. At this early stage, the villagers were already behaving toward the captive as a full-fledged member of a kinship group. Once adopted, there was no stigma attached to not having been born originally in the group. By the tenets of Iroquois society, it was considered bad form even to make a reference to the fact.

> Now you of our nation, be informed that such a person, such a family of such families have ceased forever to bear their birth nation's name and have buried it in the depts of the earth. Henceforth let no one of our nation ever mention the original name or nation of their birth.[15]

In the Crouse family lore, there is indication of what may have been a skillful use of emotions by the Seneca woman who adopted Peter Crouse. According to an account given in a skit acted out at the Crouse family reunion in 1911, when the canoe carrying the boy came up river, a woman who had lost a son his age to depredations caused by the soldiers of "Town Destroyer" (General Washington) cried loudly that he be put to death as vengeance for the death of her own son. Having used this cry of blood revenge to bring attention to herself, she then changed her mind and loudly proclaimed she should be allowed to adopt him to make up for loss of her son. The chiefs held a council and decided, "We will not kill him but adopt him and give him to this bereaved woman."[16]

Once decided that the boy was to be adopted, Peter received without doubt the real affection of a Seneca mother toward her young. Adoption meant bona fide familial relationship.

> . . . the captive was always made to feel that adoption was not a mere form. Real affection, and in fact all that the heart prizes and longs after in relationship, was bestowed upon them. After the ceremony was over and a name given, they

were taught to say, "my father," "my mother" "my brother," "my sister."[17]

Encouraging the adopted person to learn proper kinship terms and significantly beginning with those of the immediate family demonstrates the desire to bestow family status and ties of affection. With a whole new set of relatives, he was "reborn" and assumed a new identity. A new name was part of the rebirth process, chosen from the clan names available at the time.

Peter Crouse was given the Indian name of Ga-no-say-yeh which, along with the less precise "Old Peter" is still used by some on the reservation as a means of reference.[18] The English translation of his name is generally given as "coiled" or "one who walks around in a circle like a dog before lying down." This is not necessarily descriptive of Peter but is more likely a matter of the availability of the name at the time he was adopted. The true significance is in the giving of the name rather than the literal meaning.

What transpired between Peter Crouse and his new mother is not known. An informant on the Allegheny Reservation has stated that no one alive now knows the name of the family or the clan that adopted Peter.[19] Whoever she was, it can be assumed she bestowed on him the love of a mother who has regained her son.

The love of a Seneca mother for her adopted white child is evident in an account given by "Old White Chief" to Reverend Asher Wright, Christian missionary among the Senecas at Buffalo, New York.

> The last I remember of my mother, she was running, carrying me in her arms. Suddenly she fell to the ground on her face and I was taken from her. Overwhelmed with fright, I knew nothing more until I opened

> my eyes to find myself in the lap of an Indian woman. Looking kindly down into my face, she smiled on me, and gave me some dried deer's meat and maple sugar. From that hour I believe she loved me as a mother.[20]

The white captive Horatio Jones also taken by Seneca warrior during the American Revolution, was likewise shown tenderness and affection by his Indian mother. Jones told how she furnished him with new moccasins, deerskin shirt and breeches after he successfully ran the gauntlet and how she was very proud of him.[21]

When the American Revolution ended, the Indians were required by treaty agreement to surrender all white captives. Often this became an emotional trauma for both Indians and captives; especially for those who had been captured when young, the return to white society was reluctantly done and sometimes they had to be physically dragged back. In some cases they escaped at the first opportunity and returned to the Indians. The Moravian missionary John Heckewelder from Bethlehem made the observation that adopted captives:

> . . . are so kindly treated that they never wish themselves away again. I have seen even white men who after such adoption were given up by the Indians in compliance with the stipulations of treaties, take the first opportunity to escape. . . and return. . . to their Indian homes.[22]

Tenderness and affection for an adopted family member was not limited to the foster mother alone. There is evidence that Jones' foster father was also strongly attached to his new son. The Indian father could not be persuaded to give him up despite great pressure by a British subject who offered monetary reward and invoked the name of the king.

> . . .A British officer wanted to purchase Jones - having bought two prisoners of the same family before. The Indian father refused the offer, because Jones was his adopted son. The officer offered gold and told how rich his father, the King, was. "Go and tell your father the king that he is not rich enough to buy Ta-e-da-o-qua" (Jones) replied the Indian.23

Jones apparently also felt a strong emotional attachment to his Indian parents and his new life in the forest. It was a much freer life, allowing him to engage in his favorite activities of hunting, fishing, and being close to nature.[24] Not surprisingly, Jones refused to go back to white society and like Peter Crouse became a skilled woodsman and fisherman among his adopted people.

A formal statement of the power of adoption on the Indian mind can be seen in a letter by some important Senecas to the State of New York dated November 21, 1798.

> The Sachems, chiefs, and warriors of the Seneca Nation, to the Sachems and chiefs assembled about the Great Council fire of the State of New York.
> Brothers, This Whirlwind (American Revolution) was so ordered and directed by the Great Spirit above, as to throw into our arms, two of your infant children, Jasper Parrish and Horatio Jones.[24]

There is then repeated the statement made by Farmer's Brother during the Six Nations Council Meeting at Genesee River in 1798. /See footnote 11, Chapter 1 in which he tells of their great affection for the captives./[25]

The chiefs and warriors at Buffalo Creek Reservation gave long and careful thought to the whole matter of adoption and its impact on their society. One of their white captives had been very successful and in recognition of this had been named chief. He had several sons who also were named chiefs. This caused "Old White Chief" to worry that some of the Indians might feel too much distinction had been accorded his family and resent this fact. He told some of his "relatives" about this concern and that perhaps he should leave the Indians. They were much upset at the possibility of his leaving and called a council of chiefs and warriors. After a long deliberation, it was evident they did not want "Old White Chief" and his sons to leave.

> We cannot give up our son and brother, nor our nephews (White Chief's sons). They have lived on our game and grown strong and powerful among us. They are good and true men. We cannot do without them. We cannot give them to the pale faces. We shall grow weak if they leave us . . . We need their wisdom and their strength . . . We know they will honor us.[26]

The Seneca adoption tradition fit in well with the highly developed political structure of the Senecas and with their kinship system which was intertwined with the political. A very effective method of social control had evolved over the centuries through a system of checks whereby political power was moderated by kinship ties and clan loyalties curbed by political affiliation.

Even though it is not known today what clan Peter Crouse was adopted into, what is certain is that he was immediately drawn into the kinship network of the Senecas and as a fully-accepted adult became politically influential.

There is a good possibility he was brought

into the Wolf clan. A number of references to his being a member of Chief Cornplanter's household, notably that made by Reverend Alden, could mean that he had been adopted by Cornplanter's clan (Wolf) or had married a "Cornplanter" woman. (Professor Wm. Fenton feels his Indian name sounds like a Wolf clan name.)

During an interview with Mrs. Dema Crouse Stoffer, great-great-granddaughter of Peter Crouse, she stated that Peter married a Cornplanter woman before marrying the Onondaga woman with whom he had eight or nine children.[27]

In a geneology of Peter Crouse made by Professor William N. Fenton, this wife, Rachel, is listed as a member of the deer clan.[28] This would mean that due to the Seneca tradition of matrilineal descent, Peter's children belonged to the deer clan. His sons' children, however, belonged to the clans of their mothers so that today Crouse descendants are spread throughout the various clans.[29]

A modern example of Seneca adoption can be seen in August 24, 1940 ceremony of adoption for Governor Arthur H. James of Pennsylvania. It has not been recorded whether the governor saw this as anything other than an obligation of his office but the Indians took it seriously. According to Congdon, it was handled by the Cornplanter Indians with Alice White chosen to be the governor's mother. He mentions that Alice White was for many years a leader among the Indian women at Coldspring village.[30]

The modern "political" adoption such as that of Governor James is not typical of the Senecas as it is inspired usually by group interest where as the traditional concept was that of an individual right. In a letter to Lewis H. Morgan, dated October 27, 1874, Reverend Asher Wright, writing from the Cattaraugus Reservation, states:

> The right to adopt other persons is said to have been strictly an individual right. Anyone might take an outsider as his brother or other relative, and by so doing, cause him to become a member of his clan.[31]

The exercise of an individual right which kinfold must accept could be a disruptive force in a society were it not used with restraint. In Seneca society two important restraints were in effect. One, that it was exercised by the women only and thus presented no great problem within the politics of the matriarchy; second, that it helped "maintain the maternal family unit as the dominant and primary social unit, for the person adopted was first adopted into the family.[32]

A white captive taken by the Senecas the same year as Peter Crouse was Luke Swetland of the Wyoming Valley area of Pennsylvania. Indian raids in that area had caused enough concern to make General Washington discharge forty men from the Continental Army in January 1778, who lived in that area, so they could protect their families. Luke Swetland was one of these forty men and they built Forty Fort, Pennsylvania.

On August 25, 1778, Luke and a neighbor were captured by Senecas and taken to a village near present-day Geneva, New York. Luke told of his adoption and acceptance within the system of kinship:

> I was given to an old squaw as a grandson. She made a great lamentation over me, showing many signs of respect. In her family were three little squaws, who did the same. . . the captain of the scouts . . . told me how I was disposed of, and how they called their relations in their way, told me, 'This old squaw is your grandmother,' and pointing to the biggest of the little ones, said, 'This is your sister, and these two little ones, your cousins.' And so he went on through

> the town, telling me who were my relations, saying I would soon be an Indian myself; then would know all about it . . . so I became settled in Appletown.[33] [present town of Romulus, Seneca County, New York State]

The notorious Simon Girty was also adopted by Senecas, but like Horatio Jones, he had to run the gauntlet first. Girty, who was taken captive with his family in 1756, was successful in going through two rows of Indians wielding clubs and sticks. His reward was a ceremony of adoption which he said ended in a brook with three young Indian women in a ritual of purification whereby they symbolically washed his white blood away and renewed his veins with Seneca blood.[34]

The adoption tradition as used by a non-Seneca had an important effect on the Seneca people. Mrs. Asher Wright, wife of Reverend Wright, became very concerned about destitute Indian children who often were brought to her door in desperate need of food, clothing, and medical attention. As a clergyman's wife, Mrs. Wright did not have the financial resources to help the Indian children as much as she wished to help them. Both Mrs. and Reverend Wright sent out appeals for help and they were successful in getting support from a number of people, especially a Quaker named Philip Thomas. Thus, in the latter half of the nineteenth century this hard-working couple who had pledged their lives to help the Senecas touched a strong Seneca value and in 1855 founded an institution that was to serve the Indians well into the next century. Mrs. Caswell, also serving on the reservation, wrote:

> Encouraged by promises of aid from this good man, Mr. and Mrs. Wright received into their own family ten sick and starving Indian children. . . Thus began. . . the Thomas Orphan Asylum for destitute Indian children . . . upon the Cattar-

augus Reservation.[35]

Mrs. Caswell has written that she found on a monument in the old Indian burying ground in Buffalo, New York, a touching comment on the Indian practice of adoption.

> A faithful history of all the captives who have been taken by the various Indian tribes, and adopted and grown up among them, would form a very interesting volume; and if such a record could be placed by the side of the record of Indian wrongs faithfully delineated, it may be doubted whether the comparison would not be greatly in favor of the Indians, so far as humanity is concerned; notwithstanding all that has been said and written of the cruelty of savages.[36]

With adoption came complete socialization of the new member. Full participation in the society was open to the person adopted. No role was forbidden because of past affiliation or of racially different origin. Potential achievements included positions of power and leadership, including that of chief.

Peter Crouse was never named chief as was "Old White Chief" of the Buffalo Reservation but he became a highly respected and influential member of Seneca society. This did not occur because as a captured white child he promoted culture change among the Senecas but rather because he was given the chance to learn the skills and values of the society and was welcomed into that society as a full-fledged participant.

> . . . the degree of receptivity of a culture depends . . . on social values and attitudes, and on institutions to mediate the induction of alien individuals into it . . . in some societies, such as these Indian ones highly re-

ceptive to transculturites, it is difficult for an alien individual to remain periferal except as a guest, or visitor or trader. To live *in* them he must in a sense be "reborn" into them.[37]

For a number of years after the laconic military communication of 1778 noting the slaying of Peter Crouse's father and the capture of young Peter, there was no record of the existence of Peter Crouse until the notation made by Maclay in 1790 and the fuller reference made by Reverend Alden in September 1816.

Reverend Alden's account is particularly valuable in that it not only documents Peter Crouse's existence but also tells us that the former captive boy had grown up to be a man of family and influence in the Indian community. In his letter to Reverend McKean, he tells how happy he was to find shelter at the Crouse cabin after riding all day in a cold rain and then gives what is probably the best description known today of Peter Crouse.

> . . .Our host, a German by birth, was taken in the Revolutionary War at the age of fourteen years and was adopted as one of the Seneca tribe. He appears in the Indian costume and with his ears slit. His habitual language is that of the soft, melodious, and truly lonick Seneca; yet he is able to converse in the English, and a little in his vernacular. His squaw is a well-behaved, neat, and industrious woman, and they have a numerous family of fine looking children. He gladly received one of our bibles. . . Although he cannot read; yet his children are learning, and he expressed the hope of one day profiting, through their aid, by the contents of this sacred book.[38]

Peter Crouse's successful adjustment to living in the Indian community was evidenced by signs of prosperity such as large fields and an impressive house.

In addition to hosting the missionizing President of Allegheny College, Reverend Alden, Peter also made welcome the Philadelphia Quaker, Halliday Jackson. Mr. Jackson and his associates Joel Swayne, Henry Simmons, John Pierce, and Joshua Sharples were sent to the Allegheny Reservation by the Philadelphia Yearly Meeting to help the Indians. After having met with the Indians and their leaders and told them they wished to teach them how to plow, sow, and reap, Jackson noted in his journal of 1798-1800: ". . . and after these sayings were ended the Chiefs and Rulers of the people went a part unto the house of Peter*" (*a white captive)[39]

Praise for Peter's hard work and industry are found in an account written by Mrs. M. F. Trippe, wife of a missionary to the reservation. In an unpublished manuscript, which she said she wrote after "forty-five years of valued acquaintance with the Crouse families" she commends the captive for "wisely adapting himself" to the conditions of his new environment.

> His habits of life are not recorded by word but by broad well-tilled acres and by a large building of beautiful squared logs which until a few years ago was still to be seen on the flats north of Onoville . . . .the building was of unusual proportions, probably 30 x 46 feet, large for an Indian home.[40]

This structure referred to by Mrs. Trippe was later used as a hay barn and stood for many years in testimony to Peter's hard work, industry and skill with a broad axe.

In a letter from Abel Pierce, son of Hannah Crouse, the captive's fourth daughter, to Mrs.

Trippe dated May 30, 1929, we learn that Peter built an additional residence after the large log cabin referred to in most accounts.

> When Peter Crouse first came here he lived in a small cabin down on the bank of the river where the late Henry Huff's place is now. In a few later years he built a house by the Main Road where he died.[41]

Agricultural pursuits were not all that Peter Crouse excelled in, as he is also remembered for great ability in field and stream. Congdon makes a reference to him as a great trapper and riverman.

> He used to follow trapping in the season when the fur was good. He would take his canoe and go down the river as far as Oil Creek and sometimes be gone months, trapping muskrats and otter. When he came to an otter slide and they had gone away he could tell which way they had gone. . . Sometimes the white people would ask him how he could tell. Well, he would say, you have your trade and this is mine.[42]

The Warren County Historical Society (Penna.) had a copy of the Trippe manuscript in which on page 3 there is a footnote #2 which reads:

> There are plenty of words which attest Peter Crouse's worth--deeds, affidavits, etc. which have come to light in the early records of Warren County. He was also a very successful rafter and lumberman.[43]

Despite old age and sickness, Peter continued to follow the ways of forest and stream. When he became so severely crippled with arthritis that he found it difficult to walk, he continued to get around by boat on the river, pushing himself along with poles.

Congdon notes that Joseph Elkington (Superintendent of the Quaker School) wrote in his diary in 1834 that he paid a visit to Peter Crouse.

> . . . an aged captive confined to his bed for two years, crippled but gets around fishing in a little canoe. His wife is an Onondage; many children. Peter respected by both whites and Indians. Looks like an Indian. His ear being cut and hanging loose as is the case with many of the old Indians.[44]

. . . "Wilderness life among the natives had its pleasant side," declares Arthur C. Parker, himself a Seneca and an author of a book on Seneca history.

> It was an unhappy experience for those who would not or could not adapt to Indian way of life. If the captive made the effort to change, then his life would take a happier turn. Once the captive began to look for the sunny side of aboriginal life, he generally found it enjoyable. This was so true that it was frequently almost impossible to persuade captives to return to civilization. . .[45]

Peter Crouse was one of several white captives among the Senecas as a result of the Revolutionary War. In her writings, Mrs Trippe places the number of captives at seven. Mrs. Trippe relates that Mrs. Laura M. Wright, who arrived as a missionary to the Buffalo Creek Reservation in 1832, was her source of information and that Mrs. Wright knew most of them personally.

Mrs. Trippe makes reference to Mary Jamison, Peter Crouse, White Boy Pierce, the brothers Seneca White and White Seneca, the Snyder boy, for a total of six specifically mentioned. One could add to this list Jasper Parrish, Horatio Jones, Lashly Malone, Elijah Matthews, Nicholas Tanewood, and Nicolas Rosencrantz to bring the total to twelve captives held by the Senecas during the Revolution. Of these, it was declared that "Matthews, Rosencrantz and Krause were married to squaws."[47]

Although so many captives adapted so well to Indian life, there were painful adjustments to be made. The problems of a different language, food, and clothing were of great magnitude but within the close relationship of family and clan could be easily overcome. Relationship with the outside community could be a greater problem. The respect the Senecas held for adoption tradition protected the captive from torture and execution and, in some cases such as Peter Crouse's, even from running the gauntlet. However, considering the ferocity of the violence which occurred on the frontier, it is not surprising some residual animosity showed itself toward a white captive on occasion.

No incident of animosity has been recorded in the captivity of Peter Crouse once his adoption had been agreed upon. Either he was very fortunate or the incidents were never serious enough for anyone to have taken note of them. In the case of "Old White Chief" however, there is a very specific racial reference in an incident related to Mrs. Wright.

> As I grew older I sometimes excelled in the foot race, and I well remember that on one occasion when I outstripped all the other boys . . . One of them said, 'I don't care, he is nothing but a white boy!' I immediately hung my head and ran from the playground to my mother and hiding my face in her lap, I cried bitterly and loudly . . .She took me in her arms and said, 'Well, my son, it is true - you are a white boy. You can't

help it, but if you always do right and are smart, you will be none the worse for belonging to that wicked race. Whatever you undertake, do your best and the Good Ruler will bless you.[48]

That Peter Crouse was held in high respect by Indians and whites we see ample evidence. Some of this high esteem is seen through records and some in folklore.

There is on record a notation that in 1818 the Western Missionary Society of Pittsburgh was concerned that the school for Indian children which the Society had started in 1815 was not going well and that "Mr. Law was appointed to write to Peter Crouse on the above subject."[49] Two years earlier, Peter Crouse had been asked to witness a deed dated November 22, 1813 from Chief Cornplanter to Joseph Mead. The deed is in the possession of the Warren County Historical Society Warren, Pennsylvania.[50]

It is fitting that Peter Crouse, having spent so much time fishing and traveling by small boat in the area, should have his name given to a geographical landmark. A small stream which flows into the Allegany from the east, and a short distance upriver from Onoville, bears the name "Peter's Creek."

As a person who was both Seneca and white, Peter Crouse was well-qualified to serve as an intermediary between the two groups. A pay voucher in the amount of $75.50 from the United States Government, signed by the commanding officer at Fort Franklin attests to his value as an interpreter. The voucher, dated 1st March 1793 is for services rendered as "interpreter to the Garison (sic) of Fort Franklin from Octr. 1st 1792 to Feby. 28th 1793 Inclusive, 151 days a Half a dollar pr. day."[51]

Other instances have been noted where Peter

Crouse served as a go-between or interpreter between Seneca and white. It is mentioned by Congdon that Reverend Asher Bliss "visited every house (on the reservation) with Peter Crouse as interpreter.[52]

A reference is made to him and to his son, also named Peter, in a report made by a Quaker committee on Indians. The December 17, 1835 report states:

> Peter Crouse (an adopted Indian) we did not see, he being absent on a trapping excursion, but with his son (Peter) we were much pleased, he is a well educated young man and formerly had charge of the school at this place and appeared disposed to resume it, the first opportunity if sufficiently encouraged . . . we encouraged Peter again to open school as soon as the contract expired with the master now there, and he gave us some expectation that he would.
>
> signed Robert Scotton
> Thomas Wistar[53]

The minutes of the committee also state in a November 30, 1836 report that a council of chiefs was held and "present were Robinson, Black Snake, Ino Pierce, Sky Pierce, Jacob Jameson, Tunis Halftown, Wm. Patterson and sixteen or eighteen not chiefs. Peter Crouse to interpret." According to the listing in the index this was Old Peter.[54]

Peter Crouse is listed as one of the important people on the reservation by a former white neighbor of his named Charles Aldrich. Aldrich, who later moved to Iowa, reminisces about his early life on a farm located two miles from Coldspring, Cattaraugus County, New York.

> We used to see many of the Seneca Indians in those days . . . The noted Chief Corn-

> planter or Gi-ent-wau-kie lived some fifteen miles south of us . . .father . . .attended his funeral . . .when he died in 1836. . .I remember many other prominent Indians of this tribe . . . There wer Gebusk, Little Philip, John Titus, Dan Kilbuck, King Pierce, Governor Blacksnake, Tandy Gimerson, Old Buck Tooth, Jim Bucktooth, Little John Buck Tooth, John Shambo, Peter Crouse, Old Johnnie Watts, Old Thief Thompson and many others.[55]

It is interesting that Aldrich, who was very important in the founding of the Iowa Historical Society, sould include Peter Crouse as not just an important person on the reservation but as one of the important Indians.

An important indicator of mutual acceptance for a newcomer in a socity is that of marital acceptance. The evidence strongly shows that Peter Crouse and other white captives were fully acceptable as marriage partners.

Peter had found no difficulty in securing marriage partners and neither did his descendants. When Mrs. Trippe wrote her manuscript in 1928, she set the number of descendants of Peter Crouse at five hundred and sixty-six.[56]

Intermarriage of children of white captives took place mostly with Indians but there were instances where children or grandchildren of captives married descendants of other captives. This appears to have taken place between Crouse and Jameson progeny.

> Peter R. Crouse, an educated intelligent half blood, is a resident at Cold Springs; his wife is a granddaughter of Mary Jemison. His father, then a boy of fifteen years old, was taken prisoner during the border wars of Pennsylvania, conformed

> himself to Indian habits, married a squaw, and spent his life, as a matter of choice, among his captors.[57]

From time to time, there have been reunions by descendants of Peter Crouse for purposes of socializing and celebrating their common history rooted in the exploits of their famous ancestor.

Probably the most elaborate and well-known of these get-togethers was that held on September 16, 1911. In the beautiful setting of a chestnut grove on the banks of the Allegheny River, the proud descendants of the white captive watched a dramatization of the life of Peter Crouse. Beginning with his arrival as a frightened young boy and his adoption by a Seneca woman, the skit re-enacted Peter's meeting with Chippany, the "Witch's daughter" and his subsequent marriage to her. Chippany's mother had sought refuge with her clan at the Allegany reservation after having been threatened with death on the Onondaga reservation for supposedly being a witch. With age and maturation as a family man, Peter is depicted as a wise counselor and friend to Indians and whites alike, living a long life of peace and contentment on the reservation.[58]

The reunion of 1911 was of sufficient importance and magnitude to invite the interest and comment of local newspapers. The September 12, 1911 issue of The Republican Press of Salamanca. New York, commented under the headline of "Big Indian Celebration." They noted Peter Crouse's success in the Seneca way of life:

> With the help and inspiration of his able wife, Peter became a large landholder, a lumberman of large interest, a fur trader, and the keeper of the Raftsmen's Inn. Often he went down the river to Pittsburgh. Though he was invited many times he would never return to his white relatives. His intense love of his woodland

home, of his good wife and bright children were ties that held him to his adopted people and these were too strong to admit of a break. His life was one noted for his strength of character and his descendants today are men and women of sterling merit.[59]

The process by which a non-Indian became an Indian through acceptance of the Indian way of life has been termed "Indianization." On the frontier it was readily understood that some aspects of behavior on the part of the new settlers had to change for survival benefits. However, where the connection could be made that wearing buckskin clothing and coonskin hats, making canoes and dugouts for travel, and planting corn were imperative to living in the wilderness, the adoption of the Indian way of life in total was looked upon with mixed feelings by the whites.

> To the Puritan mind it was only right in the cosmic scheme of things that the Indian should become civilized and Christianized or perish. No wonder, then, that to Indianize voluntarily was tantamount to a crime.[60]

Compounding this "crime" was the emotional aspect of Indianization on the part of both Indians and non-Indians. It came as a shock to the white community when at the end of the Revolutionary War white captives such as Peter Crouse refused to return to white society. True to their part of the bargain, the Indians forced themselves to give up their captives but white relatives were dismayed when many of these Indianized captives resisted the return. Hallowell comments of this bewilderment:

> . . . the lack of understanding by relatives and others of the psychological depth of the emotional ties Indianiz-

ation may bring about and the consequences of a blind demand for captives' redemption.[61]

Professor Hallowell, quoting Henry Beston (1942) goes on to say:

> The Indian path had its own gods; it was strong medicine. Those who had followed it and were later returned to their own white inheritance, often heard the shaking of the Indian rattle and voices of Indian ghosts. I remember the man from Wells who all his life sat on the floor like an Indian and maintained that they were better people than the whites.[62]

One nineteenth-century writer who was struck with this phenomenon of Indianization of captives concluded there were many reasons for this preference but the most important was the kindness shown to them and their full acceptance in Indian society. Speaking from personal observation of the Senecas in the Buffalo, New York area:

> . . . The author in his boyhood has listened to the recitals of captive whites among the Senecas, and well remembers how incredible it seemed that they should have preferred a continuance among them to a return to their own race. . .young when captured, is partly to be accounted for in the novelty of the change--the sports and pasttimes--the 'freedom of the woods'--the absence of restraints and checks, upon youthful inclinations. But chiefly it was the influence of kindness, extended to them as soon as they were adopted. The Indian mother knew no difference between her natural and adopted children; there were no social discriminations. . .they had all the rights and privileges in their tribes, nations, confederacy, enjoyed by the

native Iroquois.[63]

A review of the events of Peter Crouse's life indicates most certainly his full acceptance into Seneca life and culture. He became an integral part of the Seneca people in whom he found the joys, security, and complete feeling of belonging. No individual could ask for more.

FOOTNOTES

CHAPTER 2

[1]William Adams, Historical Gazetteer and Biographical Memorial of Cattaraugus County, New York (Syracuse, N. Y.: Lyman Horton &Co., 1893), p. 105.

[2]Timothy Alden, An Account of Sundry Missions Performed Among the Senecas and Munsees, (New York: J. Seymour, 1827), p. 11.

[3]Boyd, loc. cit., p. 25.

[4]Merle H. Deardorff Collection MG 220(Pennsylvania Archives)

[5]Thwaites and Kellogg, loc. cit., Footnote 55, p. 212.

[6]Samuel McLay, Journal 1790 (Williamsport, Pa.:John F. Meginnes, 1887, p. 32.

[7]Draper Manuscript, Vol. 4S, p. 112.

[8]Lewis H. Morgan, League of the Iroquois (Secaucus, N. J.: Citadel Press, 1972), p. 339.

[9]George S. Snyderman, Behind the Tree of Peace (Philadelphia: University of Pennsylvania, 1948), p. 23.

[10]Draper Manuscript, Vol. 17F "The Livingston Republican" newspaper clipping (Genesee, New York, May 29, 1879).

[11]Donald H. Kent and Merle H. Deardorff, "John Adlum on the Allegheny" Pennsylvania Magazine of History and Biography, Vol. 84, p. 458.

[12]Pennsylvania Archaeologist, Vol. XVIII Fall, 1948, No. 3-4, pp. 79-80.

[13]Arthur C. Parker, The History of the Seneca Indians (Port Washington, N. Y.: Ira J. Friedman, Inc. 1967), p. 50.

[14]Snyderman, loc. cit., p. 20.

[15]Ibid., p. 14.

[16]From a copy of the program, Crouse Family Reunion at Onoville on September 16, 1911. Program in possession of Dema Crouse Stoffer.

[17]Harriet S. Caswell, Our Life Among the Iroquois Indians (Boston: Congregational Sunday-School Publishing Society, 1892), p. 60.

[18]when I mentioned doing research on Peter Crouse to a Seneca on the Allegheny Reservation, he said "Oh, yes, old man Crouse, Ga-nó."

[19]Letter of August 11, 1974 from Mr. Leo C. Cooper, Kill Buck, New York past president of the Seneca Nation.

[20]Caswell, loc. cit., p. 53.

[21]Draper Manuscript, Vol. 17F, loc. cit.

[22]John Heckewelder, History, Manners and Customs of the Indian Nations (Historical Society of Pennsylvania, 1876), Vol. XII, p. 218.

[23]Turner, loc. cit., p. 289.

[24]Ibid., p. 290.

[25]O'Reilly, loc. cit., Letter dated November 21, 1798.

[26]Caswell, loc. cit., p. 55.

[27]Interview with Mrs. Dema Crouse Stoffer at her home on Allegheny Reservation, June 6, 1972.

[28]Unpublished Crouse geneology chart, Fenton Holdings, 1933.

[29]Cooper, loc. cit., Letter of August 11, 1974.

[30]Charles E. Congden, Allegany Oxbow (Little Valley, N. Y.: Straight Publishing Co., 1967), p. 122.

[31]American Anthropologist October 27, 1874 letter of Rev. Wright to Lewis H. Morgan, Vol. 35 1933. p. 144.

[32]Pennsylvania Archaeologist Vol. XVIII, Fall 1948, Nos. 3-4. p. 80.

[33]Edward Merrifield, The Story of the Captivity and Rescue from the Indians of Luke Swetland (Scranton, Pa., 1915), pp. 21-22.

[34]Boyd, loc. cit., p. 34.

[35]Caswell, loc. cit., p. 110.

[36]Ibid.

[37]A. Irving Hallowell, "American Indians, White and Black: The Phenomenon of Transculturation," Current Anthropology Vol. 4, No. 5, December 1963, p. 528.

[38]Alden, loc. cit., p. 112.

[39]Halliday Jackson, Journal to the Seneca Indians Vol XIX, p. 132.

[40]M. F. Trippe, Mrs. Unpublished Manuscript, Historical Facts Concerning Peter Crouse, the Captive, His Wife Rachel, Their Descendants and Their Times.

[41]Deardorff, loc. cit., Letter from Abel Pierce to Mrs. Trippe, dated May 30, 1929.

[42]Congdon, loc. cit., pp. 69-70.

[43]Volume at Warren County Historical Society, Warren, Pa. "Cornplanter Grant" Seneca Grant.

[44]Congdon, loc. cit., p. 70.

[45]Parker, loc. cit., pp. 150-151.

[46]Trippe, loc. cit.

[47]Deardorff Collection, quoting p. 159 Alfred Hindelsoper in Memoirs of HSP, Vol. IV, Part 2, Philadelphia, 1850.

[48]Caswell, loc. cit., pp.53-54.

[49]Congdon, loc cit., p. 70.

[50]Ibid.

[51]Deardorff Collection, Wayne Papers XXV, 131.

[52]Congdon, loc. cit., p. 76.

[53]The Minutes and Papers of the Indian Committee from 1795-1815, Vol. II, (Philadelphia: Quaker Archives) p. 285.

[54]Ibid. p. 317.

[55]"Recollections of the Senecas" Annals of Iowa, Vol. VII, April-Jan 1905-1907, Series 3, DesMoines, Iowa, pp. 380-381.

[56]Trippe, loc. cit.

[57]Turner, loc. cit., p. 510.

[58]Congdon, loc. cit., pp. 72-73.

[59]The Republican Press, Salamanca, New York, September 12, 1911.

[60] Hallowell, *loc. cit.*, p. 525.

[61] *Ibid.*, p. 521.

[62] *Ibid.*, p. 525.

[63] Turner, *loc. cit.*, p. 46.

CHAPTER 3

SENECA CULTURAL VALUES

Peter Crouse's life with the Indians was profoundly affected by the cultural values of the Seneca way of life. As a forest people, the Senecas were closely attuned to nature and the seasonal cycles of "earth mother." Their cultural priorities involved the need to keep the forces of nature beneficial and friendly and to develop individuals within their society who understood the natural order of things and their own role within that prescribed order. The twin bastions of the Seneca were nature, with its various manifestations, and the superbly developed and controlled individualist who could function within the cosmos.

In the enculturation of its youth, one sees the carefully designed process which produced the desired individuality in both males and females of Seneca society. An individuality that would carry the Senecas through years of misfortune and adversity and enable them to survive to present day stronger than ever.

> Even today the underlying methods used for indoctrinating the children with the values and skills of the tribe remain. . .essentially the same as they were prior to white contact. Jesse Cornplanter informed W. N. Fenton that the education of the boy never stops--his mother 'takes charge' until he is big enough to accompany the men folks in their quest for game and finally able to join a War expedition. The father is then the leader.[1]

While the child is growing and learning, Senecas are very indulgent and tolerant toward his or her behavior. Children are taken to various social functions and encouraged to participate.

Fathers will often have a young boy by the hand as they dance in the longhouse to the sound of drum and rattle. The moving signt of a public confession was even more awesome on one occasion when a member of the longhouse admitted to past misbehavior in the presence of hundreds of onlookers, while a young son clutched his father's hand and stared at him in disbelief.[2]

It is not only males who are involved in the dancing with children at the longhouse. An important part is played by the women.

> . . .clan matrons and the older women dance with the children of other women during the mid-winter festival. . .their educational methods were the timeless ones; example and precept, reward and punishment. The Iroquois boy learned largely by doing and his schooling began long before adolescence--his play was by nature a training for future life.[3]

Traditionally Indian families were small so there would not be many sisters and brothers within the immediate family. When children did come or were "sent by the Creator" in Seneca thought, there was great rejoicing and the children very much loved. The famous Indian writer, Parker, himself a Seneca, points out:

> Children were greatly loved . . . the coming of a child was an occasion of rejoicing and girls were even more welcome than boys, since the female occupied an honored place. Nevertheless, each family had only as many children as it could properly care for, which was seldom more than three, even birth control being a right of mothers. . .[4]

It is a tribute to Seneca culture that individualism was so desired and prized that it produced men and women of strong will and character but who were also courteous and considerate to others.

> There is a large part of the Indian mind which cannot be explored by a white man. There are things about Indians we cannot appreciate. . . . Take the matter of courtesy, for instance. The Chinese and the Senecas have a more delicate sense of natural courteous conduct than the average Anglo-Saxon-Celtic-Romance Dutch American.[5]

John Heckewelder, a zealous missionary to the Indians from the Moravian Church of Bethlehem, Pennsylvania, was very favorably impressed with the courtesy and respect the Indians showed to others and to themselves. Heckewelder was so impressed he termed it a "reverence for each other" that he found astounding for a so-called uncivilized people. Although not "civilized" in the opinion of the white settlers, he says he found them actually civil to each other.

> I do not believe that there exists a people more attentive to paying common civilities to each other than the Indians are . . . In more than one hundred instances, I have with astonishment and delight witnessed the attention paid to a person entering the house of another.[6]

Other writers have commented on the extraordinary courtesy of the Iroquois, of which the Senecas as the most numerous of the five-nations confederacy illustrated most vividly.

Francis Parkman, writing in the latter half of the nineteenth century, noted:

> . . . a kind of courtesy . . . tended

> greatly to keep the Indians in mutual accord . . . the Indian bore abuse and sarcasm with an astonishing patience . . . In his dread of public opinion, he rivalled some of his civilized successors.
> All Indians, and especially these populous and stationary tribes, had their code of courtesy, whose requirements were rigid and exact; nor might any infringe it without the ban of public censure. . .[7]

The Seneca individualist, developed through immersion in his or her culture, was also a person of great dignity. People who journeyed to the Indian lands as traders, trappers, surveyors and government agents were often surprised to find highly principled, courageous, loyal and intelligent human beings instead of the lowly savage they expected.

One of the finest men ever produced by the Senecas was the great chief Gy-ant-wa-kia, known as Cornplanter to the whites. It was his difficult duty to steer his people around the shoals and riptides of the American Revolution. Somehow he managed to keep the Senecas from being totally scattered and crushed by the upheavals of that period and then when it was over, through personal friendship with George Washington, even succeeded in getting part of the Seneca lands back.

Peter Crouse's first wife was a Cornplanter woman and for a time he lived in the household of that great chief. As a white man trying to learn the ways of the Indian, he was fortunate in having so distinguished a model to follow. The Commonwealth of Pennsylvania was so favorable impressed with the qualities of Chief Cornplanter that it gave him a grant of land in perpetuity and when he died, erected a monument in his honor.

The monument is the first known to be

erected in this country by any public authority to any Indian . . . a sincere tribute to an unlettered Indian who, in the words of the monument's inscription, was 'distinguished for talents, courage, eloquence, sobriety, and love of his tribe and race.'[8]

Another outstnding Indian of the time of Peter Crouse was the famed orator Red Jacket. In this individual we see the distinction made by the Senecas between war chiefs and peace chiefs. As a sachem, Red Jacket's function was to propose and discuss at council meetings rather than fight military battles. His few attempts on the war path were undistinguished whereas his forays in debate and discussion were brilliant.

An eyewitness account by Thomas Morris, son of Robert Morris of the American Revolution, pays tribute to the power of Red Jacket's oratory and to his personal bearing during treaty proceedings at Canandaigua, New York in 1794.

> Red Jacket was at that time about 30 or 35 years of age, of middle height, well-formed, with an intelligent countenance and a fine eye, and was a fine-looking man. He was the most graceful public speaker I have ever known; his manner was at the same time both dignified and easy; he was fluent, and at times, witty and sarcastic; he was quick and ready at reply; he pitted himself against Colonel Pickering, whom he sometimes foiled in argument. The Colonel would sometimes become irritated, and lose his temper; then Red Jacket would be delighted, and shew(sic) his dexterity in taking advantage of any unguarded assertion of the colonel's. He felt conscious pride in the conviction that nature had done more for him than the colonel.[9]

As a preliterate people, the Senecas had to rely on memory rather than written notes or books. Anyone who aspired to be a sachem had to undergo rigid training or practice in the art of oratory. The Senecas never interrupt people who are talking as it is considered grossly impolite. One must listen carefully to whomever is speaking, marshalling his arguments for rebuttal at the same time and then when making reply be certain to give it in a dynamic style, using metaphors with incisive impact and persuasiveness.

> Nature and training had fitted them for public speaking. . . They were in fact professed orators, high in honor and influence among the people. To a huge stock of conventional metaphors they often added an astute intellect, an astonishing memory, and an eloquence which deserved the name. . . They had no art of writing to record events . . . Memory, therefore, was tasked to the utmost, and developed to an extraordinary degree . . . In conference nothing astonished the French, Dutch, and English officials, than the precision with which before replying to their addresses, the Indian orators repeated them point by point.[10]

A very important Indian who lived at the same time as Peter Crouse on the Alleghany was a half-brother of Chief Cornplanter named Ga-ne-o-dí-yo or Handsome Lake as he was known to the whites. He lived in the Cornplanter household, as Peter Crouse did during his earlier years, and was in the shadow of his brother's eminence until June 1799.

It was at the time of the strawberry festival in June 1799 that this heretofore unknown brother of Cornplanter had a religious vision. The impact of this experience was one of personal and individual reform for the prophet and for his followers.

There is an emphasis on individual responsibility and behavior.

> The "code" reminds one of the Koran. It is a disjointed collection of several hundred pronouncements made by the prophet at various times and set down later by his disciples . . . emphasis on sobriety, industry, and domesticity translated into terms they could understand.[11]

Seneca individualism is seen in their political structure and government. Nothing in the operation of tribal or federal councils could be coercive or detract from the individual's concept of right or wrong.

> The wild man hates restraint, and loves to do what is right in his own eyes. There was little in all the framework of the government of the Iroquois of restraint or coercive laws. . . And this principle extended in a great degree to family government. Their children were reproved, not injured or beaten, and none but the milder forms of punishment ever resorted to.[12]

Seneca values concerning the worth and dignity of the individual brought about a concept of the proper relationship between government and the individual that is different from any which developed in Europe. Regarding the guiding principles of the Iroquois Confederacy, Fenton notes:

> What uniquely distinguished it from European government of the time was the dignity accorded the individual . . .every individual in the confederated nations had to the right of being heard and a personal interest in the proceedings of their councils.[13]

The Senecas valued individuality so greatly that they required unanimous agreement at their council meetings. Those who disagreed on an issue had to be persuaded. The Senecas rejected majority rule on the basis that the majority had no right to impose its will on those individuals who disagreed. Opposition had to be resolved and dissolved through the power of oratory and reason or otherwise the proposal must be abandoned.[14]

Friendship is very high on the scale of values of the Senecas. Heckewelder noted that where with the whites the meaning of a friend is very broad and can assume an indefinite dimension with the Indian it is different.

> The word "Friend" to the ear of an Indian does not convey the same vague and almost indefinite meaning that it does with us; it is not a mere complimentary or social expression, but it implies a resolute determination to stand by the person on all occasions, and a threat to those who might attempt to molest him.[15]

For the Indian, the concept of friend serves as a guide for his relations to others. Since he believes that good and evil are mutually exclusive to the point they cannot co-exist in the same person, he feels that a good person should see to it that evil people are avoided so as not to threaten the good which is in him.[16]

Many whites, in their contact with the Senecas, saw them as very serious, stoic, and insensitive people. They were accustomed to seeing them at conferences and meetings where their appearance was generally of a somber nature. Those people who stayed with them long enough to begin to know them as they really are recognized their humor, enjoyment of jokes, and their fondness for goodnatured tricks and pranks. Even the very serious brethren from the Moravians at Bethlehem recognized that there was a happy side to Seneca life and commented on it in their journals. A more recent comment was made by Parker:

> The Seneca were not a gloomy people, but to the contrary, a people who were fond of being excited. They enjoyed humor and jokes, and life in a Seneca town was lightened by the telling of humorous tales, and the playing of good-natured jokes.[17]

Parker also pointed out the steadfastness of the Seneca people and their successful resistance to being overwhelmed by the intruding whites. "The Seneca have proven the virility of their race. It is a stock that does not easily give way to innovation, nor will it permit itself easily to be displaced."[18]

The Philadelphia Quaker, Joshua Sharpless, was very much impressed by the strength of character of the Seneca Indians. In a notation he made while serving the Society of Friends mission on the Allegheny in 1798, there is graphically illustrated the pride and individuality of the Seneca.

> . . . An Indian man came in and presented us with about four pounds of fresh venison. . . We gave the Indian a quarter of a dollar for his venison, which he received with apparent reluctance; but as he could not speak English, we were at a loss to know, whether it proceeded from what we gave him being too little or too much. In the same afternoon he took three of us down in his canoe to Cornplanter's village. . . He took the money with him and gave it to Cornplanter telling him that the venison he brought us was a gift, and he wished not to receive any money for it, and it was handed back to us,

> but which we immediately presented
> to him for bringing us down in his
> canoe, and he received it cheerfully.[19]

Considering the awesome weight of the white invasion into their lands and their way of life, it was inevitable that some things had to be modified and that change in Seneca culture would occur. This did come about and the Seneca tree of values with its prized individuality had to bend to the powerful wind of the white man's might. But, as Joshua Sharpless noted and many others found out, the Seneca people could only be manipulated so far and then would stubbornly resist and hold on to their own traditions and values.

Israel Chapin, Indian agent for the U.S. Federal Government at Canandaigua, New York, well understood the Indian tenacity in keeping his culture when he sent a letter to James W. Henry at the War Office in Washington, D. C. on November 15, 1796. Part of the letter read: "From the long experience I have had with the Indians I am fully convinced it is much easier to make a well-bread(sic) American an Indian, than an Indian a white man, much less a Quaker.[20]

The strong-willed and individualistic Seneca was molded by cultural values to be a product of nature and a part of the natural environment. Somewhat condescendingly one writer in the first half of the 19th century pointed out "we should look on their virtues as sure marks that nature has made them fit subjects of cultivation as well as us. . ."[21]

In looking at the world around him, the Seneca did not make a strong distinction between men and animals or trees and streams, earth and stones. Everything was part of nature's plan, of which he formed an integral part. It was important to see oneself as part of this natural world and live in harmony with other creatures and objects which make up the world.

> Men and animals are closely akin. Each species of animal has its archtype, its progenor or king, who is supposed to exist somewhere, prodigious in size, though in shape and nature like his subjects. A belief . . . that men themselves owe their their first parentage to beasts, birds, or reptiles, as bears, wolves, tortoises, or cranes; and the names of the totemic clans, borrowed in nearly every case from animals, are the reflection of this idea.[22]

The Senecas have been called the children of the forest. Not only the men but also the women and children spent a great deal of their time in the deep woods, mountains, and meadows of upper New York State and the areas of the Finger Lakes and Great Lakes.

The bark walls of the longhouses did not serve as restraints to a people who were not just at home in the forest but whose home was the forest.

It is easily apparent that male adults as hunters and warriors would spend days, weeks, and sometimes months in the wilderness. What may not be so apparent is that women were also out and away from the longhouse working in the cornfields, gathering firewood, picking berries and nuts, collecting herbs and mushrooms and during fishing expeditions splitting and hanging fish to dry on racks along the shore.

As for the children, depending on their age and sex, they became an integral part of the woodland scene. From the very beginning of their actual birth, when the Seneca woman was put into a specially built hut in the forest to have her baby, the child emerged as a product of the forest. The mother returned to her village after two or three days bringing the baby with her. Symbolically, she had gone into the forest alone and returned a twosome.

If the child were a boy, he would soon join the little boys playing in the woods and fields with bows and arrows, already in training for the hunting trail and the war party. A girl would begin early to help her mother and go with the women to do their work.

Whether boy or girl, the child grew up in a world of stories, myths, or legends pertaining to creatures and spirits of the wild and their relations to humans. The child was taught to see nature as composed of many kinds of mysterious beings, forces, and powers.

> To the Indian, the material world is sentient and intelligent. Birds, beasts, and reptiles have ears for human prayers and are endowed with an influence on human destiny. A mysterious and inexplicable power resides in inanimate things. They, too, can listen to the voice of man and influence his life for evil or for good. Lakes, rivers, and waterfalls are sometimes the dwelling-place of spirits; but more frequently they are themselves living beings, to be propitiated by prayers and offerings. The lake has a soul; and so has the river, and the cataract. Each can hear the words of men, and each can be pleased or offended. In the silence of a forest, the gloom of a deep ravine, resides a living mystery, indefinite, but redoubtable.[23]

The great Seneca orator, Red Jacket, in one of his finest speeches, declared that all people were made by the same "Great Spirit" but they were made with differences. In addition to the easily observed variations of complexion and custome, there are other "gifts" which indicate differences. He pointed out that the whites had their great gift of the arts (technology) of which the Indians knew little. Can it not be concluded that the Creator gave us different religions?

> . . .may we not conclude that he has given us a different religion according to our understanding; the Great Spirit does right; he knows what is best for his children; we are satisfied.[24]

Faith and confidence in the work of the "Great Spirit" as seen through nature were the hallmarks of Indian religious belief. Having been impressed with this aspect of Indian culture Samuel Drake writing a biography of famous Indians included in his book, published in Boston in 1832, a quotation from a poem by Sprague:

> I venerate the Pilgrim's cause
> Yet for the red man dare to plead;
> We bow to Heaven's recorded laws,
> He turned to nature for a creed. .[25]

The Seneca's deep involvement with nature as both a physical and spiritual force led to the formation of various cults and associations which felt a special relationship with certain spirits or forces of nature. Parker says there were fourteen in all including such groups as the Bears, the Otters Society, the Sisters of the Sustainers of Life, the Talkers with the Spirits, the False Face Company, the Society of the Great Sharp Point (mystic animals), and the Ancient Guards of the Mystic Potence also known as the Little Water Company or Grand Medicine Lodge of the Night Song (Ganoda). These were all voluntary associations which a person joined by applying for membership and then being accepted by that group.[26]

The Senecas were very impressed with the power of the Great Spirit, known to them as Ha-wen-ni-yu, who had control of the entire world. To the Senecas, the world was the forest situated on an island which we call the continent of North

America. In this world of nature there was also He-no, the Thunderer; Ga-oh, the wind, and many other spirits for the other components of nature such as trees, lakes, valleys, mountain, fire, rock formations, and medicine.

Reminiscing of his childhood, Chief Cornplanter paid tribute to his debt to nature for many formative experiences close to nature in the woodlands of western New York and northwestern Pennsylvania. The biographer of Indians, Samuel Drake, quoted Cornplanter as saying "when I was a child, I played with the butterfly, the grasshopper and the frogs," giving us a different view of an Indian whom we have known mostly in our history books as a prominent war chief.[28]

Cornplanter also spoke to the Quaker Missionary Henry Simmons, Jr. about his feeling of awe and affection for nature and the Creator of all the world and all things in it.

> Cornplanter informed me that when a young man, he was a great Hunter, and often thought of the Great Spirit, who made the wild beasts, and all things and to be sure he always had very good luck he said.[29]

Peter Crouse grew to manhood in the wilderness and absorbed from the forests and streams the same love of nature the Senecas felt for their homeland. There are many accounts of Peter as a "white Indian" and how he dressed and looked the part. Although Peter never joined the longhouse religion of the followers of Handsome Lake, his total immersion in Seneca culture and the many years in close contact with nature in the wild made him likewise a person of the forest.[30]

Thankfulness is the key to Seneca relationships with the supernatural. There are no words in the Seneca language to curse the gods or to blaspheme. The tradition of thanksgiving is so strong that no concept of anger or frustration toward the Creator and the forces of nature ever developed linguistically. The typical message to the spirits is a humble one of gratefulness for what has been received.

The longhouse becomes hushed as the speaker rises to the central position at the men's end of the structure. Even the children sense that some thing important is about to happen. In a powerful voice, the "sonorous tones" as Reverend Alden termed them, of the native Seneca language give forth their message of thanks to the many forces of the natural earth upon which the Senecas have been nourished through the centuries.

For several minutes the supplication continues and the Indian tobacco, thrown onto the flames showing through the open door of the wood-burning stove, brings forth clouds of gray smoke moving upward to the ceiling.

The Seneca does not pray for things the way the white man does; the Seneca does not want to seem to be telling the supernatural what it should be doing. I ask an Indian friend what the man is saying and I am told he is giving thanks for everything--the earth, the rivers, the trees, the clouds, the wind, the sun and moon, everything that has been good for our people.[31]

The kinship system into which Peter Crouse was adopted was a strong and extensive one. Once permission was granted by the chiefs for his acceptance into Seneca society, the captive was securely embraced by a system of relationships that would see to it he would be fed, housed, clothed, and protected as much as humanly possible Very quickly a captive would learn that unlike white society with its emphasis on the nuclear family, Senecas were embraced securely by the powerful clan system.

The clan was a matrilinear family or group of families having a common

> symbol and meeting in a common council . . . The clan was a political family, or a civil unit, and the right, as such a unit, to own the personal property and the rights of its deceased members. It had the right to nominate civil chiefs and of deposing them; it had the right of revenging the injury of one of its number, of torturing captives or of adopting them; it had the right of burying its dead in a common ground, and of assembling the living in civil or religious councils.[32]

The new arrival in Seneca society, whether newly born or recently adopted, would have to learn the proper way to address his relatives. In the first half of the nineteenth century, one writer found the following in general usage:

Hoc-sote = Grandfather	Nod-no-seh = Uncle
Uc-sote = Grandmother	Ah-geh-huc = Aunt
Ha-nih = Father	Ha-yan-wan-deh = Nephew
No-yeh = Mother	Ka-yan-wan-deh = Niece
Ho-ah-wuk = Son	A-ya-gwa-dan-no-da = Brothers and sisters[33]
Go-ah-wuk = Daughter	
Ka-va-da = Grandchildren	
Ah-gare-seh = Cousin	

The Seneca concept of incest was comprehensive in that no one could marry within the clan and preferably not within one of the "brother" clans. It was thought best to find one's marriage partner in one of the clans of "The other side" or "cousin clans." Seneca society being split into two parts (or moieties in the terms of the anthropologist), a person knew the clans closely affiliated with his own and those which were not as close but rather were in the opposing group.

At the time of Morgan's study of the Seneca, the "animal clans"--Bear, Wolf, Turtle, and Beaver were brother clans. The "bird clans"--Heron, Hawk, Snipe, and Deer were brother clans forming the other side or other half (or moiety). These relationships continue basically unchanged today among the Senecas except for those Indians who have become exclusively Christian and do not pay very much attention to clan affiliation.[34]

Marital choice was by personal preference, as one would expect from such strongly individualistic people, but it operated within the framework of the clan system so as not to violate cultural values regarding too close inter-marriage.

In the case of a captive, such as Peter Crouse, there could be a modification of the clan rule. Since an adopted person was not an original blood relation, a relaxation of the taboo might have taken place. So it is known that Peter lived in the household of Cornplanter, a wolf clan member, and that Peter's first wife was a "Cornplanter" woman. Peter's Indian name appears to be a wolf clan name so the possibility is there that he was attracted to someone in his adopted clan. By the end of the eighteenth century, the clan system was considerably weakened in authority and status. With his being originally white, the Indians may have seen it as of little importance. Only one child was born of this first marriage, a male named William in 1800.

Shortly after the birth of this first child, Peter Crouse took a second wife, Chippany, and their first child, George W., was born in 1807. There were eight other children: Polly in 1809, Nancy in 1811, Peter in 1813, John in 1815, Lydia in 1817, Hannah in 1820, Sally in 1822, and Nicholas in 1825.[35] All the children were given Christian names, typically the Crouses have been strong church members, and they have often been leaders of Christian congregations on the reservation.

Why Peter Crouse left his first wife is not known. It is possible she died and he married Chippany, whose Christian name was Rachel, to replace her. It is likewise possible they did not get along and in Seneca fashion easily broke off the relationship.

> Marriages among the Indians are not, as with us, contracted for life; it is understood on both sides that the parties are not to live together any longer than they shall be pleased with each other.[36]

In the Seneca tradition, children belong to the clan of the mother. Whether the father stays with them or not, the clan is the controlling factor in the child's naming, status, loyalty, and identity.

> . . . the child always belonging to that of his mother. Each clan had the right of nominating all the officers pertaining to that clan . . . Each clan had its own set of titles and personal names, which descended from generation to generation. . .[37]

Each clan had its own lists of names to be used as the occasion arose. There were children's names, adult names, and, very important, there were the sachem names for those clans so entitled. A person discarded his "baby name" when the adult name was bestowed, generally at the time of the strawberry festival in June. A man honored by his clan with a sachem's name was known by that name as long as he lived, provided he fulfilled the duties of his position properly. If he did not meet his obligations in the eyes of his clan, he was warned or if severe enough the name and office taken away from him.[38]

> In all these matters the old women of the clans took the lead, so that it used to be said they could put up or put down whomsoever they chose, and they could approve or veto all the acts not only

> of the councils of their own clan but those of the tribal and national councils also . . .[39]

Reverend Asher Wright goes on to emphasize the exclusive ownership of clan names by stating that they were never interchanged among the clans and that they were "inviolable property." [40]

Kinship concepts influenced the housing of the Seneca in that a number of women who were related to each other would occupy a multi-household dwelling known as the longhouse. These women were usually part of a lineage of one clan, with husbands from the cousin clans. The children always belonged to the mother's clan so they became part of that lineage already established in that particular longhouse. In this respect, the children were as permanent as their mothers, grandmothers, aunts, uncles, and cousins but not their fathers. Males who were living in the longhouse because of a marital alliance were in a non-permanent situation. The house and the corn stored in it belonged to his wife's clan. One's clan does not change through marriage so his allegiance and loyalty were still to the clan he was born into--that of his mother. He had no claim of ownership to anything in his wife's longhouse other than personal property he had brought in himself.

> Usually, the female portion ruled the house . . . the stores were in common, but not to the luckless husband or lover who was too shiftless to do his share of the providing. No matter how many children or whatever goods he might have in the house, he might at any time be ordered to pick up his blanket and budge. After such orders, it would not be at all peaceful for him to attempt to disobey. The house would be too hot for him; and unless saved by the intercession of some

> aunt or grandfather, he must retreat to his own clan; or, as was often done, go and start a new matrimonial alliance with some other.[41]

A man who moved out of the longhouse occupied by his wife and children might go back to his mother's or move into another longhouse with a new wife but he did not forget his children. Although he no longer lived with them, he would still be interested in their well-being and they recognized him.

Especially in the case of male children, the father followed their growing up and took an active part in training the boys for their future adult occupations of hunter and warrior. This was done on a level of close friendship and camaraderie. A father never disciplined a child. If this should be necessary, mother's brother would perform that duty. Indian children were very rarely inflicted with corporal punishment. Usually mothers controlled their little ones adequately with oral admonishment, looks of disapproval, or stories of what happened to bad children when evil spirits heard about them. The Senecas felt that if a father struck his son, something would be irreparably damaged and lost between them. Children were too valuable to be misused. The Indians were shocked at the way whites beat their children and that some white males would father children and not concern themselves with them any more.

> They informed me of one of their Women who had a child by a White man who then resided at Pittsburgh, and never came to see anything about his Child - they thought the Great Spirit intended that every Man should take care and maintain his own Children.[42]

The power of the matrilineal lineage is seen in the restraint which it placed on the political system. In addition to naming the males to office, the clan maintained a continuous evaluation of each member's performance in and out of office. Promising young men were closely watched as to their potential and achievement as they matured. Seniority in age was important but a brighter younger man might gain the edge if an older brother or cousin were over-confident, lazy, unreliable, or not serious enough toward preparation for office. If the clan mothers erred and it became evident they had made a mistake, there was an institutionalized procedure for rectifying the error. Parker points out that after three warnings a chief could even be assassinated and his death not avenged by his relatives.[43] Reverend Asher Wright gave testimony to this power of the matrilineal clan of the Senecas.

> The women were the great power among the clans, as everywhere else. They did not hesitate when occasion required "to knock the horns off the head" as it was technically termed of any of the chiefs, and send them back to the ranks of the ordinary warriors. The original nomination of the chiefs also always rested with them.[44]

There were times when some males chafed under the yoke of the women's veto power and would have liked to modify this practice. No less a personage than Chief Cornplanter tried to convince the Senecas that this should be changed. The great chief was quickly squelched on this point by a Seneca woman who insisted the women keep this perogative on political issued includ- that of making war. She warned of the consequences otherwise:

> Mrs. Chitty-aw-dunk in reply told him (Cornplanter) and all present that the Great Spirit had given that power to their ancestors, and it was handed down to them from time immemorial, and they

> would not relinquish their right, and that it was given to them by the Great Spirit to prevent madmen and fools from doing mischief, that if they went to war without their consent, they could have no success, and the Great Spirit would punish them for it . . .[45]

The Seneca tradition of clan responsibility extended to any quarrels or dispute within the clan that were a threat to the kinship group and could not be resolved by the immediate family. The emphasis was not on punishment but on restoring harmony within the group. The approach was positive rather than negative in that its aim was to bring satisfaction to the person or persons who felt aggrieved rather than punish or label someone a criminal. In those cases where there was serious injury or homicide involving different clan members, it was out of the hands of any one clan and became a matter of concern to all.

> . . . the whole community became interested to prevent the discord or the war which might arise. All directed their efforts, not to bring the murderer to punishment, but to satisfy the injured parties by vicarious atonement. To this end, contributions were made and presents collected. Their number and value were determined by established usage. (Among the Huron, the price was higher for a woman's life because of her procreative function, forty presents for a woman, thirty for a man).[46]

The kinship system was all embracing from the very young to the very old. In contrast to American society today where the old are often shunted aside and made to feel unwanted, the Senecas showed great respect to the elderly and looked after them with great care and affection. There were things for the elderly to do so they could retain their dignity and sense of accomplishment.

Men too old for the hunt and war party often turned to making of tools and utensils and their wisdom was appreciated in council and parley. Women, as they became older, assumed increasing importance in the matrilineal system until as the oldest woman in her lineage, she would be at the pinnacle of power as a clan mother.

> There is no nation in the world who pay greater respect to old age than the American Indian. From their infancy they are taught to be kind and attentive to aged persons, and never to let them suffer for want of necessaries or comforts.[47]

The death of an individual brought forth the final act of kinship. The individual having always belonged to the clan, the clan reverently and affectionately must now dispose of one of its cherished and prized possessions. Before the coming of the whites, the Senecas had practiced the custom of placing the body of a deceased person on a raised platform to dry out and decompose exposed to the elements. By the beginning of the nineteenth century, the Senecas in most cases had adopted the custom of burial "in the bosom of our mother the earth." An elderly informant told Reverend Wright that in ancient times when the village moved, the bones of the deceased relatives were not abandoned but were moved right along with everyone else. Relatives were not discarded even when dead!

> Whenever, from the failure of their planting grounds or for any other reason, there was a general removal to some new location, the remains were disinterred and taken away to the new settlement where, in some conspicuous place, the bones were assorted and laid together, skulls with skulls, ribs with ribs, arm bones with arm bones, etc. etc,

> but indiscriminately as to clanship, in as compact a form as possible, and a mound raised over the bones, after which they were never disturbed. This custom, too, has been long obsolete.[48]

This ancient practice of moving the bones was revived in the mid-1960's when the Senecas living in Cold Spring and Old Town area of New York State were forced to move due to the building of the Kinzua Dam on the Allegheny River near Warren, Pennsylvania. The federal government agreed, as part of the settlement with the Seneca nation, that all Indian graves below the flood mark of 1,365 feet elevation would be moved to higher ground.[49]

Peter Crouse's remains were among those moved to a new cemetery near Sunfish Road, off old New York State Route 17. At the new cemetery, called Hillside Haven, there is an area known as the "Old Town" section where Peter lies buried today. The captive, whose first contact with the Senecas had been an enforced boat ride up the Allegheny River from Pittsburgh, was given another involuntary ride in 1965 (one hundred eighteen years after his death) on a truck from the "Old Town" cemetery to his new resting place.

In talking to Leo Cooper about this last episode in Peter Crouse's relations with the Senecas, Cooper recalled vividly the opening of the grave and the splendid condition of the bones even though the coffin had long since rotted away.[50]

The Seneca kinship system, with its emphasis on clan and lineage, entailed a clear-cut differentiation between male and female roles. The traditions and values of the group provided the young with many cues as to what adulthood would mean for them, depending on their sex.

Little boys were to grow up as fierce protectors of the longhouse and as such were not to be curbed in their spirit or daring. They were to shun menial tasks and concentrate on those activities which developed stamina and endurance for the hunt and warpath. . .

> . . . children, especially boys, are not held to work; the latter are to become hunters. They are allowed their own way . . . They follow their own inclinations, do what they like and no one prevents them, except it be that they do harm to others; but even in that case, they are not punished, being only reproved with gentle words. Parents had rather make good the damage than punish the children.[51]

Honor and virtue were impressed upon the Seneca boys so that they would grow up to be men worthy of their clan and tribe. It came as a surprise to some whites that these so-called unlettered savages could exhibit powerful personal attributes and strength of character without having read a book or a bible.

> . . .cruel and unmeriful as they are, by habit and long example in war, yet whenever they come to give way to the native dictates of humanity, they exercise virtues which Christians need not blush to imitate.[52]

The men were not completely idle if not at war or hunting. In addition to spending considerable time at such tasks as fixing their gear, sharpening tools and weapons, they pitched in to help in those heavy tasks in which men excel due to greater muscle power than women.

Heavy work such as building a new house or adding to an existing one to make room for a newly married girl was a job for the men working together as a team. Also, the clearing of a field for planting by girdling the trees and then burning them was done by the men. Bark from the trees would have been split off while still green and with poles and logs go into the making of a new home.[53]

Once the house was built, however, it belonged to the women and the males carefully avoided work that had to do with the maintenance or running of a household within. They could be expected to fix the roof if it rained but not tend the fire or go out of the house to gather firewood.

> The husband never offers to put wood on the fire, except it be that he has guests or some other extraordinary call to do it, for the woman cuts the wood and brings it to the house and is, therefore, the proper person to take care of the fire.[54]

When the Senecas were at war, the role of the war chief was the paramount one for the males to aspire to achieve. This came about as the result of a long apprenticeship as a neophyte attached to a group of older and experienced men who were willing to take him along and instruct him in the ways of the warpath. After becoming an experienced veteran, he might achieve enough status to cause others to volunteer to follow him as a war leader. When he became a leader of leaders through success and personal charisma, he reached the lofty heights of war chief.

> War chiefs Cornplanter and Brant (who was a Mohawk) exercised controls because of their dynamic personalities. . . . During periods of comparative peace, the civil authority gradually resumed controls relinquished during the war periods. At no time was their authority given up permanently.[55]

The civil authority was really the clan functioning through the clan mothers and represented at the council by the sachems or peace chiefs. The sachems were men of great respect, dignity, and oratorical ability. They had come up through the usual training and conditioning for young males as their individual respect from others had to come through boys' games and sport in the field. They would have taken part in some war party activity but usually their potential as speakers would have brought them to the attention of the clan mothers who carefully monitored the activities of the young. The women knew that the effectiveness of their power was greatly influenced by their choice of sachems, especially as these orators would be speaking for them.

> The duties of sachems were clearly distinguished from the war chiefs. And there was a speaker for the warriors and another for the women, who held the strings of office firmly in hand. . . Red Jacket. . .performed as speaker for the women during much of his career. . . (also) Handsome Lake and Ely S. Parker were educated for the council fire as sachems. . .[56]

Where the Seneca boy knew that he would grow up to be a fierce protector and provider of meat for the longhouse, the Seneca girl was quickly made to realize that as a woman she would have a vital role not only in the maintenance of hearth and home but also in the political functioning of the society.

Seneca women controlled a most basic aspect of their society in that they not only owned the children but also made the decision as to how many they would have.

> It was the rule that the control of life should be in the hands of the women and they deemed it best to bear children only when the last child was able to walk and in a measure care for himself, which was at about the age of

four or five.[57]

A woman could augment her own procreative powers through adoption of children. This might be to increase her family, or as in the case of Peter Crouse, to replace a child that had died. For whatever reason, adoption was one way for a woman to achieve greater status and expand her power within the matriarchy of Seneca society.

> The status women had as the leaders of the family was increased and expanded by the process of adoption. They manipulated this social process as they saw fit--they not only did the adopting but had the unquestioned right to initiate it.[58]

The small-size families of the Seneca came as a surprise to whites who came into contact with the Indians in the eighteenth and early nineteenth centuries. At that time, the prevailing size of American families in white society reflected the patriarchal-agricultural concept of many children to help out in the family farming enterprise. It is not surprising, therefore, that the Moravian missionary, John Heckewelder, noted in his writing that Indian women are not as prolific as the white race in that they seldom have more than four or five children.[59]

Small families cannot be attributed to an avoidance of marriage by Seneca women. An adult woman was supposed to take a husband not long after she reached the status of womanhood and most generally she did. Should the husband die, a respectable period of one year was supposed to elapse before remarriage as it was believed his soul would go to the other world after that period of time.[60]

The Seneca woman played an important part in the training of youth for adult responsibility. In addition to the training given the girls for their future role in Seneca society, the boys were also given some early lessons in how to become a good Seneca.

> . . .until the youth was old enough to accompany men on war and hunting trips, they were largely under the tutelage of their mothers or grandmothers. We have Captain John Decker's (a famous Seneca warrior) detailed description of the cold water method used by his grandmother to make him 'tuff' and a good swimmer to boot. More recently Jesse Cornplanter told Dr. William N. Fenton that the mother was in charge of the boy's education until the boy was old enough to accompany the menfolks to war.[61]

The women's interest in the young boy's education was not all rough and tough activity. Tenderness and affection helped curb youthful excesses that might hurt reputations in the future, in a society that put heavy emphasis on getting along well with others. Though he should be a ferocious and efficient hunter and warrior, among his own people he should be easy to get along with, generous, and able to join in the fun and frolic of good-natured joking. At the festivals he was expected to be a hearty participant and a good dancer.

> Children are not excepted from any of the normal activities of the group and teaching the children is not only a duty and a responsibility which adults are expected to assume but is also a 'blessing' or a 'good thing' for the adults . . .clan matrons and the older women dance with the children of other women during the mid-winter festival.[62]

Hard work was part of the role the Seneca woman played in her society. Visitors to the villages of the Senecas were favorably impressed by the industry and energy displayed by the women. In contrast, it seemed the men were much less involved as they were usually between hunts or military compaigns and remained aloof from menial tasks of the home. To the Quaker Joshua Sharpless visiting the Indians in 1798, it seemed shocking that the men were so idle while the women worked so hard.

> . . .while the men were spending their time in idleness, or shooting with their bows and arrows at a mark, a very common recreation with them, pitching quoits, jumping, playing at some kind of games, and on musical instruments. I have not while in this village seen either man or boy at any kind of work. . .[63]

Another visiting Quaker from Philadelphia commented on what also appeared to him a severe disparity between the work done by Seneca females and that done by Seneca males. Halliday Jackson observed, while on a mission to the Senecas in 1798, that it was the women who worked in the cornfields and not the men. Since a major part of the Quaker effort was to show the Indian how to engage in profitable and improved agriculture, a critical factor was the persuading of Indian males to do farm work. The Quakers found it hard to understand why the Indian males in Seneca society did not turn to the plow and work the land as the whites did.

The Quakers, and most whites of the day, did not understand the cultural barriers that existed in the Seneca value system that made farming an undesirable undertaking for a male. In the eyes of the Senecas, it was women's work to cultivate fields, not men's work. A male felt humiliated if he were to do this. Consequently, although a white captive such as Peter Crouse could feel at home behind a plow and be a successful farmer, most Seneca males were not so inclined and incurred the displeasure of the Quakers trying to help them.

In 1798, Halliday Jackson wrote that while the women were hard at work in the cornfields, " . . . the men were standing in companies sporting themselves with their bows and arrows and other trifling amusements but none of them were seen assisting their women in the labours of the field.[64]

In addition to working in the fields and doing household tasks, Seneca women were also skilled artisans in such things as basketmaking, sewing crafts, tanning of skins, and making of blankets. Heckewelder was very impressed with the warmth and durability of the blankets, made from feathers. He also was favorably impressed with the fact that old women in particular delighted in doing this kind of work and thereby showing their continued usefulness in the society.[65]

The hard work done by the Seneca women may appear unduly harsh by today's standards but was probably not that much harder a role than that of the colonial housewife of the day. Wives of homesteaders on the American frontier certainly put in a full day's work in their daily routine. A white woman such as Mary Jemison did not find the Seneca woman's role impossible or unbearable. Parker points out that she probably suffered no more hardships as a captive among the Senecas than she would have among her own people on the frontier.[66] The fact that she chose to remain with the Senecas would seem to indicate she saw the woman's role among the Senecas as more attractive than the role of the white frontier woman.

A young woman entering into a marriage relationship was taking a further role within the matriarchal kinship framework of the Senecas. She would continue doing many of the same things she had been doing in her pre-marital routine but would now be entering the stage of an "older" woman with sons and daughters of her own. This would, however, present new problems for her and the other married women demonstrated their unity with her by a symbolic act. The women of the village provided her with firewood for an entire year as a gesture of unity and interest.[67]

While the Seneca woman's role at home was one of great importance and strength, it was the political power of these women which greatly surprised the whites of colonial America. Since white society was basically patriarchal--agriculturalist at that time, they were astounded to see women of a "lowly savage," (in their view) society wield such power. The Moravian missionary Conrad Weiser was sufficiently impressed to make note in his journal in 1748: " . . . We dined in a Seneka Town where an old Seneka woman reigns with great authority. We dined at her house and they all used us very well . . .[68]

The power of the veto was the foremost example of the political power of the women of Seneca society. Should the council be swayed into a decision or course of action which the women saw as wrong or unnecessary, they made known their opposition and invariably the men would reconsider. "If the women opposed the enterprise the warriors always gave it up, because the opposition (of the females) to any public undertaking was regarded as a bad omen.[69]

Although the Seneca warrior was very proud of his prowess as a warrior, the power of the women was so strong that even in this inner sanctum of male interests female veto power was acknowledged as supreme. Even a chief as great as Cornplanter publicly bowed to the veto of the women. Speaking at an important council meeting at Allegheny of delegates and warriors discussing the possibility of going to war again, he was recorded in 1794 by the land surveyor John Adlum as saying: "we would give you orders at once, but our great women are opposed to our going to war."[70]

The warriors could not afford to take the

female veto lightly as they very much feared supernatural vengeance if they acted against the wishes of the women.

> It is here proper to observe that if the Indians go to war without the consent of the great women the mothers of the Sachems and Nation, the Great Spirit will not prosper them in war, but will cause them and their efforts to end in disgrace.[71]

The female role in Seneca society was so structured and integrated within the fabric of kinship and politics that no great women come through to us as distinct individuals. Where there are a large number of names for outstanding and imposing males who helped shape Seneca history, no such collection of female names is known to us. The counterparts to Cornplanter, Little Beard, Farmer's Brother, Handsome Lake, Red Jacket, are not apparent by name and individuality yet they were there, anonymously and collectively performing those tasks vital to the continuation of Seneca society.

> Of the unsung women who pounded corn and held the strings of office in this matriarchy we have no conspicuous examples. Yet they were: 'to whom at last all measures of public interest were sent for their approval; without which,' says Wright, 'no measure could take effect.'[72]

What greater compliment to the power and status of these women than the fact that males were required to live in the woman's longhouse upon marriage thereby having to break strong family ties of their own and that sometimes males were so reluctant to leave mother's longhouse it was necessary to bend tradition and have them continue living there after marriage.

> As to their family system, when occupying the old longhouses it is probably

> that some one clan predominated, the women taking in husbands from other clans, and sometimes some of their sons bringing in their young wives, until they felt brave enough to leave their mothers.[73]

As a forest people, the Senecas make widespread use of various products of the forest for treatment of illness, disease and injury. A variety of plant life, particularly around such places as Cold Spring, gave Seneca herbalists a large selection from nature's own pharmacy. Although Peter Crouse had left behind a developed body of knowledge regarding medicine in white society, the culture of his adoption also had a body of knowledge going back hundreds of years in its development.

Some white men , such as the Moravian missionary, David Zeisberger, have left written testimony of the effectiveness of Indian medicine.

> For many ailments they have very good remedies, e.g., for rheumatism. In respect to the affliction I have witnessed instances where they have effected a thorough cure and not only once or twice. At times they can secure desired results with only two or three kinds of roots, at other times more are required. If a simple rememdy does not afford relief, they may use twenty or more kinds of roots . . .[74]

Herb medicine for home medication continues to this day on the Allegheny Reservation as an important source of relief from various ailments. Some Senecas believe that plants were brought to the area by a people before them, possibly the people now called the moundbuilders. One Seneca has in his possession a small mortar and pestle made of stone which he claimed was used for the preparation of medicines from these plants.[75]

Very close to the home and lands of Peter Crouse was an area of extensive plant and herb life. Most of this is today underwater as a result of the building of the Kinzua Dam but it still remains a part of the legend of Seneca curing.

> . . .The run (Cornplanter Run) was a lonely and mysterious spot . . .On its banks and in the adjoining groves of pine and hardwood grew all kinds of medicinal plants . . . the Indian doctors of this band were widely famed as herbalists. On a summer day's excursion, the doctor could find white boneset (for colds), purple boneset (a diuretic), cicuta maculata (a liniment--and also a poison for suicide), elder (for heart disease), mint (for colds and bilious attacks), angelica (for pneumonia), plantain (for stomach trouble), wire grass (for warriors and ball players to use as a muscle tonic, an emetic, and a liniment), white pine and wild cherry (for cough syrup), Prenanthese Altissima (for rattlesnake bite) aspen (for worms), sumac (for measles and sore throat), Christmas fern (for consumption).[76]

Oil had been discovered by the Seneca Indians long before the coming of the white man. However, for them it was not an item associated with automobiles as we do but rather an important aid to medication. Where today we have such high quality oils as Quaker State, Kendall and Wolf's Head, using the most complet technologies for refining and processing, the Indians had their strong arms and some old blankets.

> The Indians of the Seneca Nation discovered its (oil) existence on Oil Spring reservation . . . near the

> village of Cuba. On this reservation is their famous oil spring, which they long prized for its medicinal qualities. The Indians gathered the petroleum by spreading a blanket over the surface of the spring until it became saturated with the oil, and then wrung it out and sold it as an efficacious medicine, which they properly named 'Seneca oil,'[77]

The Seneca approach to medication was not one of exactitude with carefully prescribed amounts. Their tendency was to be very generous in dosage on the theory that if something is good then an ample amount is that much better. Also, if one plant or root is not the answer, several of them used together increases the possibility of beneficial results. To the whites, this practice was unfavorably viewed. " . . . In one important respect (medically) they make mistakes, namely, in not properly measuring doses and often needlessly torturing patients."[78]

Seneca medication did not rely on physical medicine alone. They also used magical rites, incantation, sacrifices, and prayer to bring about healing. Their concept of disease was closely tied in with the idea of evil spirits and demons causing sickness through entrance into the body.

> The Indian doctor relied far more on magic than on natural remedies. Dreams, beating of the drum, songs, magic feasts and dances, and howling to frighten the female demon from his patients, were his ordinary methods of cure.[79]

Healing and medicine were of such importance in Seneca society that a number of groups and associations were formed for that purpose. Membership in these societies was highly desired and prestigious. A limitation on membership served to heighten status and the element of secrecy which surrounded the medicine societies increased the awe and respect accorded them. Usually one became eligible for membership if he had been seriously ill and then had recovered through the intercession of one of the societies. Females were generally excluded from membership but might play an important secondary role such as keeper of the false faces. Each medicine society owned certain rites, rituals, and prayers which no other group could use.[80]

Probably the best known to outsiders is the False Face Society. The members wear large wooden masks made from the live basswood tree to imitate the bodyless creatures that dance in the forest and can bring disease or can cure those who are sick. By spreading ashes in the home of the sick person, these members can induce the demon or evil spirits to leave the body of the sick person by following the trail of ashes out the door.

Not as well known to the outside world but possibly the most awesome within the group is what Parker calls the Ancient Guards of the Mystic Potence, the Little Water Company, or Grand Medicine Lodge of the Night Song (Ganoda).[81]

Only very few and guarded references are made to this group on the reservation. At Allegany and Cattaraugus reservations, the name "Little Water Society" is the common one used today. The main object of reverence is a fabulous liquid that was given to the Senecas by a supernatural being and was first used on the Good Hunter's head to make his scalp grow back again and to revive him after being dead for hundreds of years.[82]

> The Little Water Society is very old. It is the best known of all the medicine lodges among the Senecas. The power of its medicine is the theme of many marvelous stories. It will cure most any injury or wound. . .[83]

The members of this society have small amounts of the liquid in their possession, usually in a small bottle or vial. Only a drop or two is necessary for medication. The owner of the medicine has a heavy burden of responsibility toward it as there is required a rigid pattern of singing and feasting for the medicine. If the medicine feels slighted by the owner's carelessness or forgetfulness to perform the feasting and singing, then it can wreak havoc on the owner and his family. This illustrates a strong Seneca cultural postulate that with the use of power comes a weighty responsibility for the welfare of others and the society in general.

Dreams played an extremely significant role in Seneca society. In a psychological sense, the Senecas were ahead of white society in that their value system built around the dream phenomenon pre-dates Freud by hundreds of years.

Dreams were of great importance; in fact, the Iroquois part way arrived at the ideas of modern psychology. Certain dreams had to be obeyed and it was dangerous to let a lot of dreams pile up inside one's self without unloading them.[84]

In their own way, these people of the North American eastern woodlands called "unlettered savages" by the American colonists, had arrived at the concept of guilt in the subconscious. They recognized in their dream experiences secret wishes and desires which otherwise would not dare be expressed. Such importance was attached to them that "experts" in dream interpretation were eagerly sought out.[85]

> Dreams were to the Indian a universal oracle. They revealed to him his guardian spirit, taught him the cure of his diseases, warned him of the devices of sorcerers, guided him to the lurking places of his enemy or the haunts of game, and unfolded the secrets of good and evil destiny.[86]

The Senecas believed that the dream revealed

not only the dreamer's wishes, desires and anxieties but also of the other persons or spirits taking part in the dream. This dealing with the supernatural was very dangerous as it could cause harm not just to the individual but possibly also to the entire society or bring about the end of the world.[87]

Dreams caused great anxiety and worry for the dreamer, but they also have served as a means of releasing tension. The society made great demands on the individual who, especially a male, could never admit to doubts and fears. This strict role could be eased somewhat by the dream phenomenon and give the person a well-earned respite from society's strictures.

> The culture of dreams may be regarded as a necessary escape valve in Iroquois life. Iroquois men were, in their daily affairs, brave, active, self-reliant, and autonomous; they cringed to no one and begged for nothing. But no man can balance forever on such a pinnacle of masculinity, where asking and being given are unknown. Iroquois men dreamed; and without shame they received the fruits of their dreams, and their souls were satisfied.[88]

The value placed on dreams by the Senecas and other Indians of the Northeast was recognized by white traders, explorers, and missionaries. These whites soon learned that some Indians, such as Pollard, made a game of dreaming when guests were nearby so as to get what they wanted from the more richly equipped and fed. Pollard was noted for his "dreaming" of pork and run on unsuspecting whites and the great Chief Shickellamy was not above promoting some coveted item by this method.

A famous story often told is that of Conrad Weiser's visit on the Susquehanna while carrying a beautiful new rifle. The chief immediately fell in love with the weapon and promptly announced he had dreamed of such a rifle. The good missionary knew well what this meant so he handed the rifle over to the Indian. But Weiser was not to be out done. Looking at a beautiful island, he told the chief that he had dreamed he was given an island. Shickellamy had no choice but to give the missionary the island. Knowing he had been bested at his own game, he is supposed to have said to Weiser, "I will never dream with you again!"89

Seneca life was enriched by the concept of many spiritual beings. Although the whites looked down upon them as "pagans," the Indians had their own gods and spirits and a story of the creation. The Indian path did indeed have its own gods and these have been retained by the Senecas as a part of their traditional culture of the followers of the Longhouse religion. Although Peter Crouse was a baptized Christian when captured and he remained a practicing Christian all his life, the people who adopted him were a religious and devout people in their own way.

> The Seneca, however they may have differed from the Europeans in religious and moral beliefs, were not essentially immoral or irreligious. There were few precepts of an ethical nature that the missionaries could teach them, and they frequently resented the missionary attitude that they did not know what was essentially right and wrong.90

The great orator and sachem Red Jacket was eloquent, as usual, in defending his native religion. "We also have a religion," he said, "it teaches us to be thankful for all the favors we receive; to love each other, and to be united; we never quarrel about religion."91

A basic axiom of Seneca religious life was simply that Ha-wen-ne-yu was the Great Spirit or Creator whose good works and benefits should be acknowledged and appreciated by specific formal ceremonies.[92]

The Seneca did not believe in praying for things as this would appear to be interference, meddling, or criticism of the natural order of things. What was really important was to be sure the ceremonies of thanksgiving took place and that they were done correctly. In order to ensure this, the religious calendar was in the hands of a high-status group known as Ho-nun-de-yunt, or Keepers of the Faith.[93]

The Senecas surprised those whites who troubled themselves to find out about the Indian religion with a much more profound concept of god than the whites expected these stone age people to have.

> The Indian idea of God is a sublime conception. He is their tender loving father who watches the interests of his children with the care bestowed upon the infant reposing in its mother's arms. . .[94]

Actually the concept of God in the Seneca culture was not easily understood by non-Indians and the English language translates with difficulty this distinctive notion of a supreme being. The Senecas had a creator but it was not God in the Judeo-Christian tradition.

> In no Indian language could the early missionaries find a work to express the idea of God. Manitou and Oki meant anything endowed with supernatural powers. . . The priests were forced to use a circumlocution --'The Great Chief of Men' or 'He who lives in the sky.'[95]

A common error of the whites was to impose the idea of moral right and wrong on the Indian concept of God. Early writers such as Adams in his Historical Gazetteer (1893) gave a Christian interpretation and coloring to the Indian God when he wrote such descriptive prose as "holding in his hands the scales of eternal justice, which he metes out to every son and daughter of the forest."[96] Actually the sons and daughters of the forest saw all misfortune as work of the evil spirit who was the agent of disease, death, and bad events.[97]

Lewis H. Morgan was astute enough to see the Iroquois gods more in the manner of the natives, rather than have his own religious background intrude on that of the people he was studying.

> While the religious system of the Iroquois taught the existence of the Great Spirit Ha-wen-ne-yu, it also recognized the personal existence of an Evil Spirit, Ha-ne-go-ate-geh, the Evil minded . . they were brothers, born at the same birth, and destined to an endless existence. To the Evil Spirit, in a limited degree, was ascribed creative power. As the Great Spirit created man, and all useful animals, and products of the earth, so the Evil Spirit created all monsters, poisonous reptiles, and noxious plants.[98]

While the Indians believed, as did the whites that we were all made by the same creator, they were much more flexible in their thinking. The Creator, they said, made all the different races but He gave each race distinctive tasks to be done. That is what makes one peoples different from another but by no means are whites superior beings.[99]

Seneca life was greatly enriched by the rituals, dances, and festivals which were given by way of thanksgiving to the Great Spirit and all other spirits that provided the good things of life.

The festivals and dances at the Long

> House, and the meetings of the medicine societies at private houses, open with a thanksgiving speech. This varies a little with the occasion and the speaker, but it is a formal expression of thanks to the Creator for all his gifts. They are mentioned in regular order, from the ground up to the heavens: the earth, soil, rocks and water, the streams, plants, grass, herbs, bushes and trees, the wind, the sun and moon, the rain and thunder. . .[100]

Seneca religious festivals, as would be expected from a people so closely attuned to nature followed the seasons which they saw mirrored so dramatically in the forest environment around them.

The New Year's observances, which started the second full moon after the winter solstice, were the most important and lasted for nine days and nights. This used to include the sacrifice of the white dog but the outcry was so loud against it from animal lovers in the white community that it has not been known to take place since the last decade of the nineteenth century.

As winter's grip slackened and warm days began to melt the snow, the sap flowing in the trees brought sugar-making time and a festival of thanks for the renewal of life in the forest. This was closely followed by planting-time festivals and thanks for the seeds from which spring the corn, beans, and squash, and other fruits, nuts and berries that the Creator sent for his people to enjoy.

By early summer, usually the third week in June, the strawberries would ripen and the Seneca gave thanks for this first of many berries they would eat and enjoy during the coming summer months.

In late summer, when the ears of corn in the

fields filled out, one of the most important festivals of the year marked Seneca thanksgiving for the successful growth of that year's crops. Corn being such an important sustainer of life, it was given this very special thanks.

With the turning of the leaves to their beautiful shades of red, yellow and brown, the Senecas knew winter was coming and they should prepare for it. The harvest was gathered and a thanksgiving festival held to show their appreciation.

When winter came, the Senecas met the fury of an upstate New York winter with its ample snow and cold weather by relying on their stored foodstuffs and adding to them with hunting forays from their bark-covered houses. Then would come the mid-winter festivals for the new year and the words of praise and gratefulness.

> Hail, Ha-wen-ni-yu! We thank thee that we still live. We thank our mother earth which sustains us. We thank the rivers for the fish. We thank the herbs and plants of the earth. We thank the bushes and trees for fruit. We thank the winds which have banished disease. We thank our grandfather He-no for rain, We thank the moon and stars which give us light when the sun has gone to rest. We thank the sun for the warmth and light by day. Keep us from evil ways that the sun may never hide his face from us for shame, and leave us in darkness. We thank Thee O mighty Ha-wen-ni-yu, our Creator and our good ruler. Thou canst do no evil. Everything thou doest is for our happiness.[101]

The Philadelphia Quaker Halliday Jackson gives us one of the earliest references known regarding the New Year's festival and the then-still prevalent white dog ceremony. Jackson, having gone to the Allegany Reservation in 1798 was obviously not enthusiastic about the "pagan" customs he observed. As a good Quaker, the midwinter celebrations probably seemed to him to be closer to the work of the devil than a religious ceremony. In January of 1799 he mentions that he found the "heathens" celebrating one of their two major festivals, the other being the green corn festival in the summer. The Indians had erected a statue, he said, probably the good twin, and had hung the white dog on it. They than proceeded to dance, sing, laugh and make a great noise. Apparently to his consternation, as he concluded by writing "my heart was sorrowful."[102]

The statue mentioned by Jackson was that of the "good twin" a supernatural being in Seneca religious belief associated with beneficial happenings. Wooden images were erected to this mythological figure whose name was Tarachiawagon. It served as a focal point for the midwinter festival. Jackson described it as:

> . . . a wooden image of a man, round which at stated times they performed their religious ceremonies and sacrifices. The image was about seven feet in height, elevated on a pedestal, of the same block, and being pained a variety of colour, it altogether exhibited a wild appearance.[103]

Jackson seemed quite positive that the log was about seven feet tall, but some accounts give it greater and greater height until Adams placed it at thirty feet!

> . . .the Indians for many years followed the practice of collecting around a log about thirty feet long, worked into a resenblance of the human form to which they performed a kind of worship. The son of Cornplanter subsequently persuaded them to throw it into the river.[104]

Offerings were made to the spirits by the Senecas individually. It was not the custom to have professional religious practitioners as it was considered an individualistic act by a person toward the spirit or spirits to be honored. Tobacco was the most common offering, cast upon an open fire and the smoke carrying the message of thanksgiving to the spirits. Strips of meat might be burned or the white dog for public ritual at the midwinter festival.[105]

In addition to dances and rituals for showing thanksgiving to the gods, the Senecas also played a number of games as a way of pleasing the great spirit. A vigorous and out-door people, they enjoyed their sports immensely and at the same time felt a religious gratification.

> There were many popular games, and all who possessed physical ability entered into them with eagerness. The Senecas loved their pasttimes and out-of-door sports, for they had been assured by their religious teachers that these games were pleasing to the Great Spirit. To play games and to enjoy athletic skill were therefore, regarded as a part of religion.[106]

Where the white people saw a human being as a duality of body and soul, the Indians saw it as a three-part affair. There was the body, the soul and the spirit or ghost. When the body died, the soul traveled a secret path to the next world but the ghost remained near the place of burial and continued to relate to the living.[107] Burial places were best avoided in that ghosts could become upset and cause trouble for those disturbing the remains of the dead.

The Senecas did have a concern about leading a good life so that the soul could go to the other world and enjoy truly limitless existence. Reverend Asher Wright, writing in 1859, pointed out the Seneca concern for morality.

> . . .they had some notions of moral good and evil. Murder, adultery, falsehood, theft and drunkenness were regarded as crimes which would be punished after death. . . But all who abstained from these things, and especially all who were kind, and benevolent, and who were faithful to keep up the dances, and mothers who raised large families of children and childless women who brought up orphans, were sure of happiness in the spirit land.[108]

The Seneca concept of the spirit land was closely akin to the Christian concept of heaven in that it stressed a limitless from of existence that was ecstatic to the senses and posed none of the problems of existence which must be faced here in the real world. The Great Spirit wished to make the spirit world unequaled by anything a person might have experienced on the earth and a continuation of that which was delightful to limits unknown in the present world.

> . . .To form a paradise of unrivalled beauty, the Great Spirit had fathered every object in the natural world which could delight the senses, and having spread them out in vast but harmonious array, and restored their baptismal vestments, he diffused over these congregated beauties of nature the bloom of immortality . . . no evil. . . no violence. The festivities in which they had delighted while on the earth were re-celebrated in the presence of the great Author of their being. They enjoyed all the happiness of the earthly life, unencumbered by its ills.[109]

The death of a Seneca was marked by established and traditional ritual involving not only the bereavement of the immediate family but also clan response. The "other side," someone from a cousin clan, would speak for the clans and really the society in general. His remarks would be replied to by one of the clan of the deceased or a brother clan. The speaker from the other side would again address the deceased and the group at the ten-day "death feast" when the spirit of the deceased was told to go away and not bother anyone as everything had been properly taken care of. He also told the family not to mourn any longer as the ten days were now over.[110]

It was customary for the Senecas to put some prized items, food, and for a male, his weapons, in the grave so that they could be used on the trail to the other world. This practice decreased when through contact with white society, the use of coffins became widespread. However, as can be seen by this personal recollection of Charles Aldrich, the custom persisted in some cases even to the turn of this century.

> . . .Old Johnnie Watts had two boys. . . Johnnie was amiable and kind, and was about the only playmate my little brother and I had for some years. He finally fell a victim of consumption which was rife among the Indians. . . During the time he was dying the mother talked to him incessantly in their own language. . . Just outside the door the old Indian sat on a block of wood, making a bow and arrows . . . as I came in he gave no recognition whatever. . . A grave was dug after the manner of white people, and the coffin lowered with ropes. Just at this juncture Old Johnnie Watts stepped forward and dropped the bow and arrows I had seen him making. . . We understood that the family built a fire at the head of the grave every night for perhaps a week, the purpose of which was to light the spirit of the dead boy on the way to the Happy Hunting Grounds.[111]

Witchcraft is deeply imbedded as part of the

Seneca spirit concepts. Either male or female may be accused of being a witch. Even such a staunch friend and admirer of the Indians such as Heckewelder to admit that the Indians were extremely superstitious and sensitive on this subject.

> It is incredible to what degree the Indians' superstitious belief in witchcraft operates upon their minds; the moment that their imagination is struck with the idea that they are bewitched, they are no longer themselves; their fancy is constantly at work in creating the most horrid and distressing images.[112]

Witches were so feared and so revolting that once it was established by the tribal council that they were indeed so, anyone who wished could kill them and there was to be no retaliation by kin. Usually an executioner was appointed by the council to do the deed.

Peter Crouse's mother-in-law had been accused as a witch on the Onondaga reservation and had fled for her life to the Allegany Reservation. Unfortunately for her, there were a number of deaths on the Allegany Reservation soon after she arrived and she was accused of being the cause.

> Dema Crouse said that her father Sylvester Crouse told her that the mother of Chippany, who was the wife of Peter Crouse, was killed as a witch near the Longhouse at Coldspring. . .[113]

This incident mentioned by Congdon is further borne out by a recollection of John Green, first supervisor of Olean, New York, who could remember the execution of a squaw on the Allebany in 1807.

> The principal proof against her was that she had foretold that some of the Indians

> would die, who were very sick at the time. . . The execution was a horrid one; the executioner, an Indian by the name of Sun Fish, struck her on the head with a hatchet: she came to and groaned, when he cut her throat with a knife.[114]

Since Peter Crouse's mother-in-law had fled Onondaga in the hope of finding refuge with her kinsmen of the deer clan at Allegany, it is apparent that even the traditional protection of one's own clan had to give way to the hysteria of fear of witchcraft.

White society did not appear to be of any great help at the time. The Salem witch hunts had not been too long before and even in the more enlightened state of Pennsylvania laws against witchcraft prevailed. Writing in 1847 on that subject, in the Quaker Journal "The Friend," editor Robert Smith stated:

> Nevertheless, there was a law against witchcraft in Pennsylvania . . .What could have possessed the Quaker legislature of Pennsylvania at that particular juncture (1718) to adopt that old and absurb British law?[115]

Near the end of the eighteenth century and the first years of the nineteenth, approximately 1799-1801, a new force in Seneca spirituality was introduced. Centered around a half-brother of Chief Cornplanter by the name of Ga-ne-o-dī-yo (Handsome Lake) an Indian revival movement was formed. The core of this movement was made up of revelations which occurred to the prophet Handsome Lake while gravely ill and had actually died, according to his followers. The new religion combined some elements of Christianity and basically the old traditional beliefs of the Senecas. The message of Handsome Lake and the interpretations form the good word or in Seneca, the Gaiwiio.[116]

He taught repentance and good works--

> in particular temperance and conjugal fidelity. And he singled out a few of the great variety of dances for perpetuation: the four Great Ceremonies like Big Feather Dance which are central to Seneca Ceremonialism and the six stated festivals, honoring the maple, planting, strawberry, green corn harvest, and the new year.[117]

Seneca folklore is very rich, colorful. and interesting with many tales, legends, and myths. Their love of adventure and mystery coupled with a strong emphasis on spirits and the supernatural has given the Senecas a vast treasure of stories and past happenings that were told over and over again to succeeding generations. Their beginnings were lost in the haze of long ago and they will continue to exist forever.

The content of these legends and myths is filled with beautiful creatures such as the dew eagles which fly so high in the air they cannot be seen except for those rare occasions when they are spotted on the ground in the early morning mists. There are frightful creatures like the false faces who have no bodies, only twisted and gruesome faces as the carriers of disease. There are huge figures such as the husk faces; one was seen near the old longhouse at Carrolltown who appeared to be eight feet tall, according to a Seneca informant.[118] Little People also inhabit Seneca folklore; they are called Djonge-onh. and like to lurk in dark and inaccessible places. Children's tales are an important part of this legacy of myths and legends, many of them are used to help explain to children the natural world around them. Such stories as: How Bats Came into Being, Why the Robin's Breast is Red, Why the Raccoon Washes His Food and Wears a Mask, are indicative of this function.[119]

In the storehouse of Seneca myths and legends there is a myth of origin that is within the usual pattern for North American Indian stories of genesis. More correctly, it is the story of origin of a great island as the Indians have always referred to North America as an island in a large ocean.

The island was created by a big lump of dirt brought up from the bottom of the ocean by ducks and geese. It was deposited on the back of a huge turtle so that sky woman had a place to land when she fell out of the heavens.

Sky woman gave birth to twin boys, who were opposite in their behavior. One twin named Tarachiawagon was the good twin and he was a helper to mankind. The other twin named Tawiskaron was a bad twin and he did things to harm mankind. He lives apart from the world, sometimes is known as Rimdweller, and tries to do evil things when he gets his chance.

> The sons (of Sky Woman) reappear to vie in creating good and evil. One creates the various cultivated plants, herbs, and forests, and releases the game animals. His twin inflicts pain and misery. . . Of such were the fundamental beliefs and related to them were moral values of good and evil.[120]

The good twin went to live up in heaven where he looks down upon the earth and enjoys watching his people in their comings and goings. He is especially pleased when offerings are made to him and words of thanksgiving are carried up to him by the sacred Indian tobacco.

The bad twin was thrown into a pit by his brother and all malicious people and poisonous creatures are finally shut up with him forever.[121]

Thus the Seneca saw the duality of nature in the world in regard to good and evil. With legends, myths, stories, and religious sanctions, a good Seneca would find eventual reward in life after death in Seneca paradise.

FOOTNOTES

CHAPTER 3

[1]*Pennsylvania Archaeologist* Vol. XVIII, 1948, p. 46.

[2]Observed by this author at a festival held at a Longhouse festival.

[3]*Pennsylvania Archaeologist* Vol. XVIII, p.46.

[4]Parker, *loc. cit.*, pp.74-75.

[5]Congdon, *loc. cit.,* p. 101.

[6]Heckewelder, *loc. cit.*, p. 128.

[7]Parkman, *loc. cit.*, pp. xiviii-ix.

[8]*Western Pennsylvania Historical Magazine* Vol. 24-25, 1941-1942.p. 19.

[9]O'Reilly, *loc. cit.*, Personal Memoir of Thomas Morris, Vol. 15.

[10]Parkman, *loc. cit.*, p. lxi.

[11]*Western Pennsylvania Historical Magazine* *loc. cit.*, p. 17.

[12]Turner, *loc. cit.*, p. 64.

[13]Proceedings of the American Philosophical Society 1956, Vol. 100, p. 571.

[14]*Ibid.*, p. 572.

[15] Heckewelder, *loc. cit.*, p. 278.

[16] *Ibid.*, p. 288.

[17] Parker, *loc. cit.*, p. 70.

[18] *Ibid.*, p. 158.

[19] *The Friend*, Vol. XXI, 10/9/1847, p. 34.

[20] O'Reilly, *loc. cit.*, Vol. 12.

[21] Daniel I. Rupp, *Early History of Western Pennsylvania and of the West* (Pittsburg: Daniel W. Kauffman, 1846), p. 175.

[22] Parkman, *loc. cit.*, p. lxviii.

[23] *Ibid.*,

[24] Drake, *loc. cit.*, p. 312.

[25] *Ibid.*, p. 1.

[26] Parker, *loc. cit.*, p. 67.

[27] Adams, *loc. cit.*, p. 26.

[28] Drake, *loc. cit.*, p. 86.

[29] Henry Simmons, Jr., *Diary 1796-1800* Vol. 2, Pennsylvania Historical and Museum Commission, p. 2.

[30] Alden, *loc. cit.*, p. 11.

[31]Informant Leo C. Cooper, while attending a Green Corn Ceremony at the Cold Spring Longhouse Steamburg,New York, 1972.

[32]Parker, _loc. cit._, pp. 61-62.

[33]Turner, _loc. cit._, p. 56.

[34]In this regard it was revealing to be talking to a teen-age Seneca on the Allegany Reservation in 1972 who said he wished to identify as an Indian but when asked what clan he belonged to, he wasn't sure.

[35]Trippe, _loc_. _cit_.

[36]Heckewelder, _loc_. _cit_., p. 154.

[37]Proceedings of the Amer. Philos. Co., _loc_. _cit_., p. 572.

[38]Parker, _loc_. _cit_., p. 63.

[39]_American Anthropologist_, _loc_. _cit_.,p.143.

[40]_Ibid._, p. 144.

[41]_Ibid_., p. 140.

[42]Simmons, _loc_. _cit_., p. 4.

[43]Parker, _loc_. _cit_., p. 65.

[44]_American Anthropologist_, loc. cit.,p. 140

[45]Kent and Deardorff, _loc_. _cit_.,pp.465-466.

[46]Parkman, loc. cit., p. lxii.

[47]Heckewelder, loc. cit., p. 163.

[48]American Anthropologist, loc. cit., p. 139.

[49]Information received from Seneca informant Leo C. Cooper(Ha-yen-do-nees) who was head of Indian group involved in grave relocation.

[50]Conversations with Leo Cooper and field notes taken on June 6, 1972 at Allegany Reservation.

[51]Archer B. Hulbert and William N. Schwarze, David Zeisberger's History of the Northern American Indians (Ohio State Archaeological and Historical Society, 1910), p. 16.

[52]Rupp, loc. cit., p. 175.

[53]Parkman, loc. cit., p. xlix.

[54]Hulbert and Swarze, loc. cit., p. 82.

[55]Snyderman, loc. cit., p. 21.

[56]Proceedings Amer. Philos. Soc., loc. cit., p. 572.

[57]Parker, loc. cit., pp. 74-75.

[58]Pennsylvania Archaeologist, loc. cit., p. 79

[59]Heckewelder, loc. cit., p. 221.

[60]Hulbert and Schwarze, loc. cit., p. 88.

[61]Snyderman, *loc*. *cit*., p. 20.

[62]*Pennsylvania Archaeologist*, *loc*. *cit*., p. 46.

[63]*The Friend*, *loc*. *cit*., p. 33.

[64]Halliday Jackson, *Civilization of the Indian Natives* (Philadelphia: Gould, 1830), p. 29.

[65]Heckewelder, *loc*. *cit*., pp. 202-203.

[66]Parker, *loc*. *cit*., pp. 147-148.

[67]Parkman, *loc*. *cit*., p. xlviii.

[68]Rupp, *loc*. *cit*., p. 14 (Appendix)

[69]Snyderman, *loc*. *cit*., p. 23.

[70]Kent and Deardorff, *loc*. *cit*., p. 456.

[71]*Ibid*., pp. 465-466.

[72]Proceedings of the Amer. Philos. Soc., *loc*. *cit*., p. 572.

[73]American Anthropologist, *loc*. *cit*., p. 140.

[74]Hulbert and Schwarze, *loc*. *cit*., p. 55.

[75]Informant Abner Jimerson of Cattaraugus Reservation.

76Anthony F. C. Wallace, *The Death and Rebirth of the Seneca*. (New York: Alfred A. Knopf, 1970), pp. 186-187.

[77] Adams, *loc. cit.*, pp. 53-54.

[78] Hulbert and Schwarze, *loc. cit.*, p. 56.

[79] Parkman, *loc. cit.*, p. lxxxiv.

[80] Wallace, *loc. cit.*, p. 72.

[81] Parker, *loc. cit.*, p. 67.

[82] Congdon, *loc. cit.*, p. 147.

[83] *Ibid.*,

[84] Oliver La Farge, *A Pictorial History of the American Indian* (New York: Crown Publishers, Inc., 1956), p. 51.

[85] *Ibid.*, p. 53.

[86] Parkman, *loc. cit.*, p. lxxxiii.

[87] Wallace, *loc. cit.*, p. 73.

[88] *Ibid.*, p. 75.

[89] Paul A. W. Wallace, *Indians in Pennsylvania* (Harrisburg: Pennsylvania Historical and Museum Commission, 1975), p. 92.

[90] Parker, *loc. cit.*, p. 88.

[91] Drake, *loc. cit.*, p. 312.

[92] Frank J. Lankes, *The Senecas on Buffalo Creek Reservation* (West Seneca, N. Y.: West Seneca Historical Society, 1964), p. 7.

[93]*Ibid.*, pp. 7-8.

[94]Adams, *loc. cit.*, p. 28.

[95]Parkman, *loc. cit.*, p. lxxix.

[96]Adams, *loc. cit.*, p. 28.

[97]Parkman, *loc. cit.*, p. lxxix.

[98]Morgan, *loc. cit.*, p. 156.

[99]Heckewelder, *loc. cit.*, p. 187.

[100]Congdon, *loc. cit.*, p. 118.

[101]Adams, *loc. cit.*, p. 27.

[102]*Pennsylvania History*, Vol. XIX, 1952. p. 142

[103]Jackson, *loc. cit.*, p. 29.

[104]Adams, *loc. cit.*, p. 565.

[105]Parkman, *loc. cit.*, p. lxxxv.

[106]Parker, *loc. cit.*, p. 68.

[107]LaFarge, *loc. cit.*, p. 51.

[108]William N. Fenton (ed.), "Seneca Indians by Asher Wright" (1859), *Ethnohistory* Vol. 4, 1957.

[109]Morgan, *loc. cit.*, p. 177.

[110]Congdon, *loc. cit.*, p. 126.

[111]Annals of Iowa, loc. cit., pp. 381-383.

[112]Heckewelder, loc. cit., p. 239.

[113]Congdon, loc. cit., p. 93.

[114]Turner, loc. cit., p. 509.

[115]The Friend, Vol. XX, 1847, p. 209.

[116]Proceedings of the Amer. Philos. Soc. 1956, Vol. 100, loc. cit.,p. 574.

[117]Ibid.,

[118]Ernie Mohawk of Cattaraugus gave me this estimate during a conversation November 1976.

[119]From a manuscript left by Leo C. Cooper (Ha-yen-do-nees) of Allegany Reservation.

[120]Proceedings of Amer. Philos. Soc., loc. cit. p. 570.

[121]Ibid.,

CHAPTER 4

SENECA ECONOMIC SYSTEM

The economic system of the Senecas was one that developed to accommodate a new stone age people who had made a shift from a hunter-gatherer society to a horticulturalist one while retaining hunting and gathering as a subsidiary activity. Great prestige was still attached to the male hunter but the crops of the women's fields were the major sustainers of life in the longhouse.

Territorial values had been developed through their hunter-gatherer activities so that Seneca land, as such, was quite accurately marked off through reference to natural area features such as mountain ridges, creeks, and rivers. Within these borders, the land belonged to all the group for use as they saw fit.

With the horticultural development, a system was devised whereby certain fields were worked by the women of one clan, and those of other clans into other fields. It was recognized that to grow a good crop of corn, beans, and squash, a consistent effort by certain individuals identifying with that field would bring best results. This was not "ownership" in the sense that it would be fenced off to keep others out. Not only did people criss cross fields for purposes of hunting, but anyone of the group was free to move about as he or she pleased.

This kind of conditioning of the Indian toward land as a part of the economic system made it very difficult to understand what the whites meant by selling land for private ownership. The Indian felt betrayed when the people he had treated with to "sell" land then put up fences and told him to stay out.

. . .the Indian did not really understand

> white man's concept of land ownership. Land, in the Indian sense, could not be sold; only its use could be bartered. This meant that the basic ownership would remain with the Indian, and he would be free to hunt, fish, gather berries and firewood as long as he wished.[1]

Without the concept of real property and with the simple technology of a new stone age people, the Senecas did not devlop the idea of personal inheritance. Basically, a person's tools, weapons, clothing and cooking utensils were personal property and these did not change ownership through family claims at the time of death. Through the custom of a tenth day death feast, the personal property of the deceased is distributed in the form of presents.

There is a present for every person who helped in any way with the burial of the dead person and the remainder is given to friends of the deceased. After all the items have been given away, huge amounts of food and drink are given to each guest present and some gifts are set aside for special friends who were not able to attend the death feast. There is so much food that it cannot be consumed so people have prepared themselves by bringing containers for the extra food and carrying that home with them.[2]

The economic system of the Northeast Indians had developed a type of exchange which was based on seashells. The name of wampum is generally used in reference to this shell money.

> Wampum constitutes the money of the Indians. Two hundred shells cost a buckhide, or a Spanish dollar . . . Strings were made of the beads that have been strung. . .A string is usually half a yard long, sometimes longer.[3]

A more permanent economic asset than seashells

was the Seneca land itself. Although it had shrunk from millions of acres to a few thousand, what land was left to them did have some rich and fertile fields.

The Quakers sought to give the Senecas technical aid such as sawmill irons and blacksmithing tools so that the portential of the land could be used for the betterment of the Indians.

Halliday Jackson noted while on his mission as a Quaker emissary that "the land had a rich bottom, and appeared favorable for cultivation."

> . . .made them fully acquainted with the nature of the mission, that it was in order to improve the condition of the Indian natives, and to teach them the ways of good and honest white people. . .and be relieved from the distresses and difficulties to which they had been subjected by their old habits and modes of living. . . and also to example them in a life of sobriety and industry.[4]

The material culture of a people such as the Seneca was mostly concerned with the basics of food, clothing, and shelter. Trading with nearby people enabled them to have access to some specialty items such as choice stones or shells but the overwhelming majority of material goods had to come from the surrounding environment.

Being a forest people, wood was the mainstay of much of the items of Seneca craftsmanship. Wood was used for bows and arrows, for their bark houses, for mortars and pestles to pound corn into flour, for containers such as bowls, baskets, and trays, for canoes and dugouts, and for body ornaments.

Pottery in the form of small jars of several quart capacity has been often found with Seneca burial items. The use of pottery appears to decline steadily with increased contact with white society. There is a tendency to substitute the white man's kettle or to use wood containers. By the middle of the nineteenth century, Morgan observed that whereas it had been "carried to considerable perfection at an early day . . the art itself had long been disused, that it is now entirely lost.[5]

The Senecas preferred to make those items which they used every day and if possible to make them themselves. Wood was present in ample quantities, was easier to work with than stone and more adaptable. Such things as baskets, spoons, trays, bowls and combs were expertly fashioned by these forest artisans.

> . . . Herein is evidence of the innate conservatism of the Senecas, who cling to that which he himself can make and understand. . .The material culture of the Iroquois had much to do with his preservation, for it was connected with his ceremonial and ritualistic life. . .[6]

Clothing was an important aspect of Seneca culture. Although whites were fond of referring to the Indians as "half-naked," they were far from that. In the northeast woodland area, forest life and inclement weather were powerful motivations for protective clothing. Seneca craftsmanship was not content with utility alone so beautiful designs were added and a profusion of ornamental objects to enhance further the finished product.

> The Iroquois men when fully dressed wore leggings, breech-clouts, and kilts of buckskin, moccasins, and buckskin shirts. In summer this dress might be reduced to breech-clout, kilt, and moccasins. The women wore skirts and leggings in warm weather, full dresses of buckskin when it was cooler.[7]

Further protection against the cold was afforded by the use of blankets very carefully made by the women. A complex process of intertwining vines, feathers, and small strips of cedar bark produced a warm and serviceable aid against the damp and cold.[8]

The housing of the Senecas was a forest product like so many other things in Seneca life. Slabs of bark, usually elm, were cut to serve as sides and roof for the Ga-no-sote or bark house of the permanent village. Temporary housing was much smaller, usually for one family only, and used for those occasions when a family was out on an extended fishing or hunting trip.

After contact with the whites, the large multi family dwellings of the Senecas were gradually abandoned in favor of a cabin-type home made from logs. Peter Crouse built a log cabin as his first home, not a bark house. Only an important chief or sachem would have a large structure. Joshua Sharpless noted on his mission to the Senecas in 1798 that the houses were in no particular order or street but rather grouped around the residence of Chief Cornplanter.

> Cornplanter's house has two apartments; that occupied by us is thirty feet long; the other twenty-four feet, each sixteen feet wide. . . and the whole covered with a bark roof. . .They are built of round poles, let in close together by notches near the end.[9]

A society that does not have a machine technology must rely on its brawn and skilled hands to get things done. The Senecas spent many long hours making the various tools, weapons, clothing, and other necessities of life. The whites thought the Indian lazy because he wasn't doing the kind of work they did as an agricultural society. Very few whites could understand the tedious work involved in making a good bow, or the arrows or the stone points to be used with the bow and lance. Where metal tools made the work easier for the whites, the Indian might spend a whole day felling a tree by burning and chiseling over and over again.

Contrary to the stereotype the whites had of the Indians, Parker tells us that "The Seneca were a busy and industrious people, and their houses and hamlets were filled with evidences of their industrial activity.[10]

One of the most intricate and complex of the items produced by Seneca hands was the wampum belt. In making a belt, hundreds of shells had to be gathered, sorted for color and size and then painstakingly ground down to correct shape. The shells were strung on tough animal or vegetable fibre serving as a long-lasting twine.

> Strings of wampum were carried by messengers. Belts or strips of it, in various designs, were often messages or documents in themselves, and records of tribal legends and history were kept on strings of various lengths and arrangements of dark and light beads.[11]

By the time of the Quaker mission to the Senecas in 1798, a diffusion of white man's goods was already quite evident among the Senecas. Joshua Sharpless noted in being invited to eat by Chief Cornplanter that he "brought in some dinner in a bark bowl, and a tin kettle."[12]

The Senecas were lectured to by the Quakers on the advantages of industry of the type done by the whites. To men such as Joshua Sharpless and Halliday Jackson, the work ethic of the whites should be substituted for the "indolent" Indian way.

> . . .The committee let them know that the riches of whites . . were produced by industry; the men doing the work in the fields, etc., and leaving the women

> to attend to spinning, sewing, etc. in the house. . . if they were good and industrious, the Good Spirit would love them and bless them with many good things.[13]

It would seem that Peter Crouse would have been a good example to uphold to the Indians as one engaged in the kind of work that the whites did so successfully. Peter farmed a large number of acres and kept a nice family and his wife was noted as industrious by Timothy Alden. It is possible that the relative silence concerning the captive by Sharpless and others was due to the quiet disapproval by the Philadephia Quakers of his intermarriage and "Indianization." They may have been reluctant to praise him on this account.

Having been well-received at the Crouse household and enjoyed the hospitality, Alden saw fit to praise Peter's life style and his choice of wife. "His squaw is a well-behaved, neat and industrious woman and they have a numerous family of fine looking children."[14]

For a hunter-gatherer society, the land of the Senecas was a marvelously well-suited one. Many writers have attested to the abundance of game in the early years, before its severe depletion by the end of the nineteenth century. There was an abundance of deer, bear, raccoon, rabbit, squirrel turkey, wild pigeons, and many fish to be caught in the creeks and rivers.

> The men hunted deer, trapped beaver, killed duck, turkey and wild pigeons, and fished. For the fishing, they damned the streams, and worked with very large nets made of vines. . . did much of their hunting in parties.[16]

What the whites criticized as idleness was actually a seasonal fluctuation in activity by a people closely attuned to nature. The agriculturalists of the white settlements did not understand that an Indian they saw sitting around seemingly doing nothing one day might be gone for two weeks at a time with little or no food and sleep tracking game in all kinds of weather.

As the Indian lands became more and more settled, the skills of the Indians became less and less applicable. Trade goods replaced many of the hand-made items such as clothing, containers, utensils, and weapons. When Little Turtle, a Miami chief, was asked if he wouldn't be more comfortable living in Philadelphia, he replied: "I can make a bow, or an arrow, catch fish, kill game and go to war but none of these is of any use here."[17]

A relaxed people, used to nature and not to man-made deadlines, they were a puzzle even to the well-meaning and helpful who tried to change their ways. When the Quaker Joshua Sharpless asked Chief Cornplanter why they didn't plaster the cracks between the logs to make them tighter against the cold, the Chief answered that "if they made their houses too warm, they would not like to leave them when winter came to go hunting."[18]

It was not only the redman who valued the ample game in the land of the Senecas. There were some white hunters who followed the life of the food gatherer. Probably the most famous in Pennsylvania was Philip Tome.

In his autobiography, Tome tells us he was born in Dauphin County, Pennsylvania, in 1782. At an early age he became renowned as a hunter. He recalled that "at that time game, such as bears, elk, deer and wild turkeys were very plenty in that section of the country."[19]

Adams, who had mentioned that Peter Crouse had become highly skilled in hunting and trapping, mentions Philip Tome as "doubtless the first settler in Cold Spring."

> He came about 1818 from Susquehanna, Pa., and was a hunter and trapper. He caught large numbers of elk, which were abundant then. . .[20]

This meant that the Indian, who was experiencing more and more difficulty finding game was in competition with white hunters with the same interests. The overall effect was to hasten the change of the Indian economy to greater dependence on crops and livestock.

The origin of crops among the Seneca is lost in the past of long ago. There is no evidence of their ever not having crops. In a letter to Morgan in 1874, Reverend Asher Wright wrote that he asked a ninety-two year old Indian, whom he supposed to be the oldest living Seneca at that time, about the beginning of crop planting. The reply was that the Indians had corn, beans, and squash long before the coming of the white man.[21]

The Indians believe they have always had them--that they were given to them originally by their Creator, Ha-wen-ni-yuh.[22]

Very commonly, the role of domesticated plants for Seneca subsistence has been under emphasized. The adventure and glamour of hunting tend to give undue weight to this one aspect of Seneca society. Possibly the fact that males did the hunting caused writers, who themselves came from male-dominated societies, to give this auxiliary function greater emphasis than it deserved.

Corn, beans, and squash were the main food of the Senecas. This was recognized by the people themselves through their reference to the "Three Sisters" as"our Supporters."[23] Where game animals provided meat and added variety to the diet, it was the corn which was the mainstay for life. Without corn, the Senecas, the rest of the Iroquois, and all other eastern woodland Indians would have to face starvation. It was no accident that both large-scale invaders of Seneca land, Generals deNonville and Sullivan methodically destroyed the corn.

The hunting of bear, elk, deer, quail, and other animals were much more exciting both to the writer and to the hunter. It is not so dramatic to write about planting, weeding and harvesting corn. Yet this was the basis for continued Seneca life.

> Field work was done by women. In telling of that feature of Indian life, the captive, Mary Jamison, says that the labor was not heavy. The soil was sandy and loose and enriched with humus accumulated from years of rotting vegetation. Each year they planted, cultivated and harvested, working in gangs and making a social affair of it much in the spirit that women gathered for quilting parties. The yield of certain fields was reserved for tribal use at councils and national festivals, thereby relieving individuals of responsiblity for providing food for visitors on those occasions.[24]

The women did an excellent job in their tasks as horticulturists. They only asked for help from the men in the clearing of the fields. The forest was pushed aside by the slash and burn method and then the women took over. One writer credits them with raising fifteen varieties of corn and sixty kinds of beans and squash.[25]

By the nineteenth century, the number of crops had increased as contact with the whites encouraged them to add to their "three sisters." Writing in 1892, Caswell listed corn, wheat, potatoes, tomatoes, and "other products" as typical of the crops in the fields of the Senecas.[26]

Greater reliance on crops and less emphasis

on hunting and "indolence" was strongly recommended to the Senecas by the Philadelphia Quakers. These emissaries from one of the largest population centers in the colonies were adamant that the good life for the Indians would be one of agricultural pursuits.

> (the Indians). . . were strongly recommended to industry and reminded of the unreasonableness of their present practice of letting their women work all day in the fields and woods, either in cultivating with the hoe. . . or in cutting firewood and bringing it home on their backs from a considerable distance, while they (the males) were spending their time in idleness, amusing themselves with their bows and arrows, and other useless practices.[27]

Actually, the Senecas as a people knew the value of their crops in keeping them alive and well. Before the winter snows came, the women saw to it that many bushels of corn were stored under the gambrel roof of the longhouse. This would make the bread, the dumplings and the soup that would see them through until the new plantings the following year. A look at Seneca ceremonial life will show the second major festival of the year, rivalled only by the mid-winter new year renewal, to be dedicated to the green corn. There is no comparable festival to hunting and fishing. The Senecas knew that basically they were horticulturists.

FOOTNOTES

CHAPTER 4

[1]George S. Snyderman (ed.), The Manuscript Collections of the Philadelphia Meeting of Friends Pertaining to the American Indian p. 616.

[2]observed personally by the author at the death feast for Leo C. Cooper (Ha-yen-do-nees) in November 1976.

[3]Hulbert and Schwarze, loc. cit., pp. 94-95.

4Jackson, loc. cit., p. 30.

[5]Morgan, loc. cit., p. 354.

[6]Ibid.. p. 88.

[7]LaFarge, loc. cit., p. 49.

[8]Heckewelder, loc. cit., p. 203.

[9]The Friend, Vol. XXI, 1847, p. 33.

[10]Parker, loc. cit., pp. 84-85.

[11]LaFarge, loc. cit., p. 47.

[12]The Friend, Vol. XXI, p. 22.

[13]Ibid., p. 42.

[14]Alden, An Account, loc. cit., p. 12.

[15]Lankes, loc. cit., p. 4.

[16]LaFarge, *loc. cit.*, p. 44.

[17]Drake, *loc. cit.*, pp. 159-160.

[18]*The Friend*, Vol. XXI, p. 33.

[19]Philip Tome, *Pioneer Life* or *Thirty Years A Hunter* Arno Press, 1971, p. 11.

[20]Adams, *loc. cit.*, p. 485.

[21]*American Anthropologist*, Vol. 35, p. 141.

[22]*Ibid.*,

[23]Lankes, *loc. cit.*, p. 5.

[24]*Ibid.*, p. 4.

[25]LaFarge, *loc. cit.*, p. 44.

[26]Caswell, *loc. cit.*, p. v.

[27]Jackson, *loc. cit.*, p. 32.

CHAPTER 5

SENECA POLITICAL SYSTEM

Politically, the Senecas were part of an extraordinary political system which made up the Iroquois federation. They were one of the original five nations of the Iroquois Confederacy.

When Peter Crouse was forcibly removed from the jurisdiction of the American colonial system, he was interjected into a unique political entity that had developed over many centuries. The political sophistication of the Iroquois was unmatched on the North American Continent.[1]

Without having attained a written language, the components of the Iroquois system, among them the Senecas, achieved a unity and force seldom seen among a new stone age people who maintained hunting and gathering traditions concurrent with horticulture.

> Their organization and their history evince their intrinsic superiority. Even their traditionary lore . . . shows at times the stamp of an energy and force in striking contrast with the flimsy creations of Algonquin fancy.[2]

The origins of the Senecas, and the other Iroquois peoples, is one of conjecture. Their language differences suggest a migratory background as they were a linguistic island surrounded by an Algonkian sea. It is possible they moved northward from the Carolinas, after having crossed the Mississippi River in an eastward trek from the northwest coast. Political concepts could have been picked up by contact with the Cherokees, while in the Carolinas, with the Hurons when they entered the Great Lakes area.

No one knows the extent to which the Iroquois

were affected by an earlier people, extinct by the time of the coming of the white man. There has been found archaeological evidence of the "mound builders' having moved eastward from the Mississippi through the Ohio Valley and into upper New York State.

> Here, at the point where the main up-river road branches towards Bradford is the Sugar Run Site; as it now seems a series of sites of various cultures. . .Discovery of a prehistoric Indian skeleton with narrow, bulgy forehead . . .Dr. Stewart pronounced it characteristically Hopewell. . .[3]

The Senecas, and the other nations of the Iroquois, had not developed a written linear script in the manner of the whites but they did have a system of communications which functioned well in binding the far-flung groups together.

Wampum belts were more than money or items of gift-giving. They served an important purpose in transmitting long messages from one political constituency to another.

> Upon delivery of a string a long speech may be made and much said about the subject under consideration. But when a belt is given few words are spoken, and they must be words of great importance . . .A white string of felt signifies a good message and such a belt may have figures in dark wampum. . ./when/ a warning against evil, or an earnest reproof the belt delivered is in black . . ./for war/ the belt is black or marked with red, having in the middle the figure of a hatchet in white wampum. A peace belt is quite white, a fathom long and a hand broad and of not inconsiderable value.[4]

The war which brought Peter Crouse to the Senecas was also the war which would spell the doom for the military power of the Confederacy. Within a year or two after Peter's capture near Pittsburgh, General Broadhead moved upriver and destroyed corn and towns on the Allegheny river. Much more disastrously, General Sullivan marched his men through the gap at Easton, Pa. to invade New York's southern and western areas and wreak havoc on the Seneca strongholds in the valley of the Genesee and other areas.

"Last year, 1779, the Six Nations were driven out of their land by the Americans and all their towns and settlements were destroyed, a fate they had never before experienced.[5]

From 1779 onwards, the Senecas had more political expertise than political power. Very severely punished by the armies of the new republic, they held on to a small portion of their lands and tried to make the necessary adjustments to ensure survival.

During such a bleak period in their history, they were very fortunate to have a number of wise sachems and chiefs from whom they could draw confidence and resolve. Red Jacket, Farmer's Brother, Little Beard, New Arrow, and the great Chief Cornplanter were men of great wisdom sorely needed in those perilous times.

Born of a transitory arrangement between a Dutch pedlar from Albany named John Abeel and a Seneca woman, Cornplanter or Gy-ant-wa-kia, had grown to maturity in the forests of western New York and Pennsylvania. True to Seneca tradition, he took the clan allegiance of his mother--the wolf clan. As Deardorff has put it, "although he was half white, he was all Indian."[6]

> As a young men just married he had gone to his white father to ask for a "kettle and a gun." He was turned away with neither. From that time on he lived and thought as an Indian.[7]

In his long life, born about 1740 and died in 1836, Cornplanter saw the Senecas and the rest of the Iroquois Federation go from their zenith of power to their near-destruction. He was wise enough to see the realities of the times and counseled his people sagaciously. Almost singlehandedly he kept the Senecas neutral during the War of 1812 and kept them from joining the Ohio tribes who were subsequently crushed by "Mad Anthony" Wayne. It was Cornplanter who appealed in 1791 to the Quakers of Philadelphia to come teach the children those things which they must know and which they could not teach them.

> Brothers, we have too little wisdom among us, and we cannot teach our children what we perceive their situation requires them to know. We wish them to be taught to read and write, and such other things as you teach your children, especially the love of peace.[8]

This was an interesting request from a man who had achieved a great reputation as a war chief and who had thirsted for the war trail at an early age. Tradition has it that Cornplanter was anxious to get into the fight against General Braddock but that his mother wouldn't let him go because he was too young--about fifteen years old. This was verified by Blacksnake when he was asked by Draper if his famous uncle had fought against Braddock, Blacksnake said no, Cornplanter was too young.[9]

Peter Crouse, living in the Cornplanter household after his capture, saw the great chief in his capacity as peacemaker and statesman more than warrior. Cornplanter's friendship with George Washington and the awarding of a land grant to him by the Commonwealth of Pennsylvania gave him high status.

> . . .New Arrow's was much the older settlement (Old Town), and in the early 1790's official communications

> were usually addressed to (it) . . .
> The situation changed in 1795 when most of the Indians moved down with Cornplanter after his grant was surveyed to him.[10]

The Senecas received a respite when in 1784 the Treaty of Fort Stanwix was concluded. The British had abandoned their Indian alliea and friends at the conclusion of the American Revolution so the various tribes had to fend for themselves as best they could. Cornplanter was the principal Iroquois representative in this first treaty of the new American government with Indian tribes.

Under the terms of the treaty, all white captives held by the Indians were to be returned to white society. According to some sources, Peter Crouse was returned to Pittsburgh by the Indians but he was not happy there.

> I then went back to the whites and my relation and staid there a while.
> They made much sport of me. The Indians had slit my ears so they could put rings in them. They made so much sport of me in everything that I could not stand it. I went back to the Indians and married a squaw.[11]

It was a hard time for the Senecas as they tried to rebuild from the disastrous effect of the Revolutionary War on their political power and the continued loss of lands to the white greed for more and more territory.

The Senecas knew they had been defeated but they did not know they were beaten. Their political leadership under Cornplanter was seeking an accommodation that would pull them through. His call for help from the Quakers was answered and the Senecas started on the long road back to recovery.

> The once-powerful Iroquois defeated in war maintained a precarious existence, farming and hunting on their dwindling reservations, dispirited and demoralized. Strong drink was for many the last refuge. The Quaker missionary effort is unique. . . in aiming explicitly to help people in their daily lives rather than to save souls.[12]

At the same time as the Quaker mission to the Senecas, an event took place which was to have an important effect on the unity and survival of the Senecas. This was a series of revelations by the half-brother of Chief Cornplanter, a man by the name of Ga-ne-o-di (Handsome Lake). In their depths of despair and bitterness at their treatment by the whites, the Senecas now had a spiritaul and mystical rallying point. The Handsome Lake religious revival has political implications in that although only a part of the reservation became followers, its stress on the old ways and continuance of the religious festivals of the past helped maintain what Dr. Fenton has called the symbols of the Iroquois federation. A continuity was assured for the Senecas and the other Iroquois so that they were not broken and scattered to the winds. The whole structure of council and sachems remained, aided by the thrust and dynamics of a religious revival.

When Peter Crouse was adopted by the Senecas, he became of part of more than just a family. Families were not only linked to clans but clans to cousin clans and these in turn formed distinct tribal groupings. These groupins occupied different portions of the Seneca territories, whatever those happened to be at that time. All of the groupings formed the Seneca nation.

The Seneca as a nation had a common origin. Their legends told of having come out of the ground on a hill located on the east shore of what is now called Canandaigua Lake. For this reason, their name for themselves is Nun-da-wa-o-no, or Great Hill People.[13] We know of them as the Senecas due to the manner of historical contact.

> The name Seneca, as we know it today, is of Algonkian origin, coming from O-sin-in-ka, meaning 'People of the Stone.' The Dutch called all the tribes west of the Mohawk 'Sinnekars.'[14]

The Seneca nation, like the Seneca family, clan and tribe, was firmly in the control of the women. The males held the public offices, made speeches, and went to war but it was the females who controlled the decision-making. Given the tremendous independence and masculinity of the Seneca male, it is perplexing to see how this came about.

> . . .how the Iroquois woman came to exercise her many controls remains unsolved to some degree, but many of the problems may be resolved if the warriors are considered as a distinct group owing direct allegiance less to the village than to the family, and particularly to the matrons.[15]

The Seneca nation joined with the Cayuga, Onondaga, Oneida, and Mohawk nations to form the original five nations of the Iroquois. Once again historical development brought about misnaming as the work Iroquois is not of five-nations origin but rather from the French. Their own name for their federation is Ho-de-no-sau-nee and it reached from the Hudson River westward to Lake Erie. Yearly meetings were held in Central New York at Onondaga, near present-day Syracuse, New York.

> The nations . . .when assembled in general council were arranged on opposite sides of the Council fire; on one side stood the Mohawks, Onondaga, and Senecas, who as nations were regarded as brothers to each other, but as <u>fathers</u> to the remainder.

> Upon the other side were the Oneidas and Cayugas and at a subsequent day, the Tuscaroras, who in like manner were brother nations by interchange, but <u>sons</u> to the three first.[16]

Through a long cultural, and traditional evolvement, fifty sachems were voting members of the federation council of the League of Iroquois nations. These were unevenly distributed over the original five nations with nine to the Mohawks, nine to the Oneidas, fourteen to the Onondagas, ten to the Cayuga, and eight to the Senecas.[17]

These sachems had titles handed down over the centuries for each sachemship. Pine tree chiefs, men or women who had been so honored for outstanding achievement, could attend meetings with voice but no vote.

High idealism is very evident in the Iroquois federation. The Senecas and the other nations federated with them were not only well-developed politically but also held high principles and set difficult goals for attainment.

> Their outlook was directed toward definite goals of accomplishment. . .The very structure of the Iroquois Confederacy was built up on ideals. . . many of which were of amazing loftiness.[18]

One of their ideals was that of equality of the membership. Centuries before the American Revolution, the five nations adhered to the principle of political equality. One nation might have a larger number of sachems than another but by no means was this construed an inferiority on the part of the nation with fewer sachems. Things were nicely balanced out so that the Senecas, who had the fewest with only eight sachems, held both of the war chief positions.

The conferacy was based upon terms of

> perfect equality; equal rights and immunities were secured to each integral part. If in some respects there would seem to be especial privileges, and precedence, it is explained as arising from locality or convenience; as in the case of the Senecas being allowed to have the head war chiefs, the Mohawks being the receivers of tribute from subjugated nations; or the Onandagas, the central nation, supplying their Ta-do-da-hoh and his successors.[19]

The original goal of the league was to promote peace among the tribes. Rather than engage in continuous warfare, the members would respect each other's territory, help fight off outside attack, and trade peacefully with each other. In the process, they were not opposed to terrorizing non-members and enforcing a kind of Pax Iroquoia over groups on the borders.[20]

Some aspects of the Iroquois Federation were based on the same concept to be used later in the federal union of the United States of America. "The five Nations were as so many states, reserving to themselves some well-defined powers, but yielding others for the general good."[21]

Flexibility was the key to the bonds of unity of the Iroquois. Disputes did arise, bickering and jealousy did surface at times, but the federation survived. Sometimes separate wars were fought or wars that were mostly of interest to one nation, as in the case of the Senecas versus the Erie Indians, but this was accommodated within the framework of the overall organization.

> The bonds that united them were like cords of India-rubber; they would stretch, and the parts would be seemingly disjointed, only to return to the old union with the recoil. Such was the elastic strength of those relations

of clanship which were the life
of the league.[22]

Often the relations of the Senecas toward the League strained the flexibility of their bonds to the near-breaking point. The size of the Seneca nation (it was the most numerous) and wide explanse of its territory contributed to the ambiguity it felt at times toward federation. Writers such as Deardorff have visualized two nations within the Senecas rather than one; those east of the Genesee as pro-league, and those on the Genesee-Allegheny only nominally attached to the League.[23]

> At one point (c. 1750) the Iroquois on the Allegheny-Ohio were at the point of forming a secessionist League of their own. They lacked only the ceremonial equipment, principally the treasury of Wampum belts.[24]

Despite internal strains and problems, the League of the Iroquois was a formidable factor in Indian-white relations. Not only did it control a vast territory but at a time when waterways were crucial for transportation and communication it controlled the headwaters of the Hudson, Mohawk, Genesee, and Ohio rivers and the crucial areas around the Great Lakes.

Their Federation could put approximately 2,000 men in the field and move them quickly over well-laid-out trails to strategic areas. Moccasin-shod warriors moved swiftly from one area to another, carrying only a few handfuls of parched corn and some maple sugar each. Their movements were so rapid that alarmed colonists often exaggerated the number of warriors in the fields, counting the same bands many times over.

> . . .those who knew them best count the warriors at about 2,000 of which the Senecas could furnish more than half. . .[25]

> . . .the number of their warriors was declared by the French in 1660 to have been two thousand two hundred; and in 1677, an English agent sent on purpose to ascertain their strength, confirmed the precision of the statement.[26]

The political organization controlling these 2,000 or so warriors was a unique one, structured by time and tradition into a blend of hereditary and appointive powers in the offices of sachems and chiefs. Morgan refers to it as "an oligarchy composed of a mixture of elective and hereditary power."[27]

It should be remembered, however, that "elective," until the upheaval of 1848, meant that a person was placed in office by action of the council, not by election of a voting electorate.

Whatever their political processes at home, the Senecas and the other nations of the confederacy were a widely feared group in the Northeast. Parkman refers to them as a ferocious people with a government that was an oligarchy in form and a democracy in spirit.[28]

The seventeenth century was probably the peak of power for the Confederacy of the Iroquois. By the middle of that century, the Erie Indians had been crushed by the Senecas, quickly followed by shattering blows to the Hurons.

> The confederates at this time were in a flush of unparalleled audacity. . . The firearms with which the Dutch had rashly supplied them, joined to their united councils, their courage and ferocity, gave them an advantage over the surrounding tribes which they fully understood.[29]

They understood their power and domination so well that they even engaged in a practice of surveillance of nearby peoples, especially those who, although subdued, might do something not in the best interests of the League.

Peoples such as the Delawares, the Shawnees, and the Conestogas(also called Andastes) were pulling away from white incursion on the Atlantic seaboard and finding themselves on the borders of their "uncles" at Onondaga. The League went to the extent of posting an "agent" to keep watch of things in the Susquehanna Valley.

> This was Shikellimy as the Delawares called him. He was an Oneida chief. . . .Ungquaterughiathe (or) Swatane, both meaning "He makes it light for us," or "Our Enlightener."[30]

Shikellimy, faithful lookout of the Iroquois on the Susquehanna, was the father of the famous Logan of Pennsylvania border wars renown. When Shikellimy died in 1748 at Shamokin, Iroquois power had reached its zenith in New York and Pennsylvania. It began to decline not long after that as the storm clouds gathered that would unleash the American Revolution.

The dominated peoples of the federation continued to live in the shadow of the Iroquois but became more and more restless in the face of continued white settlement into Indian territory. The relentless push of the whites increased the number of diverse peoples living in the border areas such as the Ohio Valley and the upper Susquehanna.

Political strategems by the different nations of the confederacy had served to increase the power of the Iroquois. On the surface it would appear a weakness that each nation could enter into its own agreements with other peoples but in the end the outcome was otherwise.

> Thus, any nation, or any large town, of their confederacy, could make a

> separate war, or a separate peace with a foreign nation, or any part of it. Some member of the league, as for example, the Cayugas would make a covenant of friendship with the enemy, and while the infatuated victims were thus lulled into a delusive security, the war parties of the other nations, often joined by the Cayuga warriors, would overwhelm them by a sudden onset.[31]

The willingness of the Iroquois to be flexible toward defeated enemies and at the same time increase their political power is well-demonstrated in the case of the defeated Hurons.

Two principal towns of the Hurons, St. Michel and St. Jean Baptiste, had been savagely destroyed by the Senecas in a mid-seventeenth century attack that had swept everything before its path. This included the murder of French Jesuits in the towns who were administering to its Christianized inhabitants.

Those surviving Hurons who collected themselves, after the Senecas had left their towns burning and devastated, made contact with the Senecas to make a request of them.

> They. . .promised to change their nationality and turn Senecas as the price of their lives. The victors accepted the proposal, and the inhabitants of these two towns, joined by a few other Hurons, migrated in a body to the Seneca country. They were not distributed among different villages, but were allowed to form a town by themselves. . .identified with the Iroquois in all but religion.[32]

The Iroquois could play the part of the stern father when they felt any of the peoples under their wing were not acting properly, or foolishly. This was the case at an important meeting in Philadelphia in 1742 when the Onondaga Chief Canassatego rebuked the Delawares for being so foolish in their dealings with the whites.[33] The 'uncles' from Onondaga were particularly upset about the infamous "walking purchase" of 1737 in which the Delawares gave up a large tract of land.

It was the United States Government that struck the greatest blow to the Iroquois political structure. Where the Sullivan and Broadhead expeditions had crippled them militarily in 1779, the setting aside of the unanimity principle in 1797 struck a devasting blow to the political power of the Iroquois.

> . . .the general council claimed the right to prevent the sale of lands in western New York occupied by the Senecas; and would have succeeded, had not the holder of the right of pre-emption, and the U. S. Commission engaged in negotiating the treaty insisted that a majority must rule, according to white custom, and the unanimity principle of the Six Nations be set aside. At that time the Indians were too feeble (or too wise) to risk a war on that account and the tale was quickly told by the white man's bribery and whiskey.[34]

The proud and powerful Iroquois had been humbled; they had to accept political terms as best they could. The upheaval of the American Revolution and subsequent developments had rendered them weak and helpless before the white onslaught. Loss of lands, disease,and depredation almost completely annihilated a proud people who now still clung to a few acres of land and what they could salvage of their original culture.

FOOTNOTES

CHAPTER 5

[1]Parkman, loc. cit., p. xlvii.

[2]Ibid.

[3]Pennsylvania Archaeologist, Vol. XII, 1942, pp. 2-3.

[4]Hulbert and Schwarze, loc. cit., pp. 94-95.

[5]Ibid., p. 40.

[6]Western Pennsylvania Historical Magazine, loc. cit., p. 7.

[7]Ibid.

[8]Jackson, loc. cit., p. 10.

[9]Draper Manuscript, Vol. 4S, Wisconsin State Historical Society, p. 68.

[10]Kent and Deardorff, loc. cit., p. 294.

[11]Congdon, loc. cit., p. 69.

[12]Pennsylvania History, Vol. XIX, 1952, pp. 119-120.

[13]Morgan, loc. cit., p. 7.

[14]Parker, loc. cit., p. 34.

[15]Snyderman, Tree of Peace, loc. cit., p. 20.

[16]Turner, loc. cit., pp. 59-60.

[17]Morgan, loc. cit., p. 63.

[18]Parker, loc. cit., p. 61.

[19]Turner, loc. cit., p. 59. [Ta-do-da-hoh was a very high status name honoring a great warrior of long ago.]

[20]Proceedings from Amer. Philos. Soc., loc. cit., p. 571.

[21]Turner, loc. cit., p. 49.

[22]Parkman, loc. cit., p. 337.

[23]Pennsylvania Archaeologist, Vol. XVI, 1946, pp. 3-4.

[24]Ibid., p. 7.

[25]Amer. Philos. Soc., loc. cit., pp. 570-571.

[26]Turner, loc. cit., p. 42.

[27]Adams, loc. cit., p. 31.

[28]Parkman, loc. cit., p. 212.

[29]Ibid., p. 241.

[30]William M. Beauchamp, The Life of Conrad Weiser (Syracuse: Onondaga Historical Assoc., 1925), p. 8.

[31]Parkman, *loc. cit.*, p. 435.

[32]*Ibid.*, p. 424.

[33]Beauchamp, *loc. cit.*, p. 28.

[34]Fenton, *Ethnohistory*, loc. cit., p. 321.

CHAPTER 6

SENECA CULTURE IN TRANSITION

When Peter Crouse found himself hurtled into Seneca society near the end of the eighteenth century, he did not find a people in a truly aboriginal state. Although white encroachment on Seneca territory was not of any great consequence, the white man's goods and greed for furs had been affecting Seneca life for over one hundred and fifty years before the capture of Peter Crouse.

French, Dutch, and English traders had brought in their European-made goods and extracted millions of peltries from the backs of North American fur bearers. The Indians concentrated more and more on this aspect of hunting and became increasingly dependent on the whites for such newly-acquired wants as guns, powder and ball, blankets, axes, trinkets, and most ominous of all--whiskey.

The use of firearms, mostly purchased from the Dutch, and later the English, temporarily was of benefit to the Iroquois as it enabled them to establish their superiority over neighboring tribes. Blankets and axes and even trinkets were of good use but alcohol from the very beginning was an Indian tragedy.

In the struggle between the French and English for control of the North American continent, alcohol was used as a way to influence and control the Indians.

> . . .The English used one weapon, almost as potent--(in some instances more so) as Jesuit influence and insinuating French diplomacy. They had learned the fatal appetite of the Indian for strong drink, and took advantage of it, by introducing brandy and rum wherever they made their advances among them.[1]

More lasting than the evils of drink, epidemics of diseases not known before, and the loss of millions of acres of land was the physical impact of European culture on the Indian way of life. The Senecas, like the other aboriginals of North America, had to adjust or perish. A strong and resilient people, they proved they could adjust and survive although the problems are great to this very day.

Very bluntly, the Seneca were told by various whites that their only hope was to change and follow the ways of the newcomers as soon as possible. Where in white society a strong feeling of status arose for those who came before the others to these shores, toward the Indians no such status was accorded, even though they had been here thousands of years before the first white man.

> . . .When we compare the temper and customs of these people with those of our own colour, how much cause have we to be thankful for the superiority we derive from the blessings of civilization.[2]

The view held by whites that there were different levels of civilization, that some people are savages while others are "civilized" because they have writing and complex technology, relegated the Indian to an inferior status. In their opinion, any white, such as Peter Crouse, who took up the Indian way of life, was in a state of regression.

> The theory of the progressive stages of history and of the relationship of character to circumstance explained the savage's essential inferiority, the final inferiority of even his savage virtues. . .for a white person to become Indianized was necessarily a retrograde step. If the frontier farmer was a "rebellious fugitive from Society," the squaw man was doubly indictable.[3]

The Honorable J. S. Whipple, guest speaker at the "Big Indian Celebration," as the local newspaper called a Crouse reunion in 1911 honoring their captive ancestor, spoke favorably on the improvement of the Seneca people. By this he meant that they had changed their ways substantially so that they were more like the whites. He stated unequivocally: "There is nothing for the Indian to do except as the white man does; and the quicker the better for your children."[4]

The Senecas had a number of people willing to help them along on the way to becoming like the whites. Some were well-meaning people like the Quakers, others were deceitful and scheming people who wished to exploit the Indians.

> . . they are continually liable to the attempts of designing white persons, who settle, on or near their lands, for this and other purposes, and exercise a pernicious influence over them.[5]

The Quakers well understood the threat these conniving, scheming, and unscrupulous whites posed to the Senecas. They urged the Indians to remove them from their reservation lands so that their influence could be diminished somewhat. The Quaker Committee on the Indians reported they felt the Senecas recognized the danger.

> We believe many of them are aware of the baneful and demoralizing influence which the class of whites who settle among them exert over their young people, and the evils which must eventually result from it to the Seneca Nation.[6]

A letter from Secretary of War Knox written on April 28, 1792 to Messrs. Jones and Smith, Interpreters, to the five nations in behalf of the United States, demonstrates the lowly estimate of even important Indians in the eyes of government officials.

Gentlemen you are hereby appointed to conduct the Seneka Indians now in this city . . .(Philadelphia) to the Genesee Country . . . You will use your highest exertions to keep the Indians sober on the route by representing to them the disgrace and pernicious consequences of a contrary conduct. signed H. Knox[7]

While some whites deprecated and exploited the Indians, there were some others who worked hard and unselfishly to help them as best they could. The Quaker Mission to the Senecas was an example of an honest and conscientious attempt to help the Indians cope with changing times and imminent disaster. Heeding Chief Cornplanter's plea in 1791 for assistance, in 1795 there was officially organized an effort to help the Senecas.

At this time the yearly committee met to promote 'among the Indians,' the principles of the Christian religion, as well as to turn their attention to school learning, agriculture and useful mechanical enjoyments.[8]

When the delegates of the Quaker committee arrived at the Seneca Reservation at Allegany, they made known their intention to teach them the use of the plow, how to sow, and harvest so they would get a good yield from the land. It was evident the representatives from Philadelphia felt the necessity to change the Indian's traditional techniques of cultivation as they assured the Indians they would "instruct them in the use of mechanical instruments.[9]

The Senecas were woefully lacking in mechanical appliances such as were used in the white man's type of agriculture. Sticks and shoulder bones of deer were to give way to the "irons" of white society. In order to teach the Indians to keep the new tools in working order, they needed blacksmithing and mechanical expertise from outside their own group. Eventually, they would hope to develop their own skilled people. The process would take many years and in the meantime they became more dependent on white society.

> A hope was entertained (by the Quakers) that, although their improvement, at first was small, yet as they come to taste the sweets of industry, and enjoy the benefit of their labours, they (the Indians) would gradually relinquish their former pursuits and follow the example Friends were setting before them.[10]

In addition to farming, the Quakers intended to teach carpentry, shoemaking, and blacksmithing for the boys. For the girls there would be spinning, knitting, and sewing. Both boys and girls were to receive an elementary education so as to make the adjustment to white ways easier. The Quakers did not attempt to use this as a way to gain converts but rather to contribute to health, happiness, and security of the Indians.[11]

The Quakers apparently recognized the need for incentive even when something is being done for one's own benefit. According to a letter written by one of the Friends in 1798 after a visit to the Seneca reservation in Allegany, there was established a system of awards for those Indians who showed progress.

> We also proposed to encourage them (the Indians) to industry by establishing a few small premiums, to be paid under certain conditions to all such Indians in that reservation as should raise small specified quantities of divers kinds of grain, etc. and authorized our young men to pay the same under the stipulated conditions.[12]

Chief Cornplanter and other Senecas had recognized the need for change if there was to be any hope for survival. Agents for change, such

such as the Quaker delegation, were warmly greeted and there is evidence the Indians accepted the new technology and materials made available to them.[13]

While the Indians were trying to adjust and make headway, however, the press of white society onto their lands, their people, and their values continued unabated.

> And the cultivated men of the time were no less grasping than the roughnecks of the border settlement. Quite typical, or even perhaps a little better than the average, was the attitude of George Washington. . . who had been awarded 10,000 acres and who had tremendously increased his holdings by buying more from others who wanted ready money.[14]

The Senecas, like most other Indians, were very confused by the behaviour of the whites. Although they had their wise men, and Peter Crouse was included as one of their counselors, the Indians were never able to comprehend the double talk, false promises, and bold-faced lies they received from the white citizenry and officials alike. It seemed one moment they owned something and the next moment it was gone.

> . . .while it was generally admitted that territory not fairly purchased by treaty still belonged to the Indians it was also taken for granted-- by convenient mental slight of hand, that the Indians had no right to it.[15]

Indian land was subject to continued abuse by whites who trespassed at will, squatted on desirable acres, connived with corrupt government officials, and organized aggressive land companies for the sale of whatever acreage they could get their hands on.

In 1794, the great Cayuga Chief Fish Carrier had addressed the federal Indian agent General

Chapin at Buffalo Creek to protest the decision of Pennsylvania to fortify Presque Isle. After giving four strings of wampum, he told General Chapin:

> . . .we were greatly disappointed when we heard that some of our lands had been purchased without our consent and our minds have been much distressed thereof.[16]

During the time Peter Crouse was with the Senecas, there was a constant pressure by the Holland Land Company and the Ogden Land Company for more and more of what land the Senecas still possessed. Eventually, this resulted in the loss of Buffalo Creek Reservation and the moving of some Senecas to the Midwest.[17]

The Indians witnessed the rapid denuding of the forests as white settlement pushed across their former lands. Once the woodsman's axe had brought down the lofty pines and hemlock, large rafts of lumber were floated down the river to Pittsburgh. Peter Crouse took part in this and then joined in the next phase which was the agriculturist's plow.

> . . .the industrious woodsman's axe has generally been superseded by the farmer's plow, leaving the territory little else than a sparcely (sic) settled agricultural district. . .[18]

Seneca contact with people of European background exposed them to a different kind of family structure than the heavily clan-related one of their own. The white colonists, traders, and trappers who pushed into Seneca territories were of the small, nuclear family background and maintained this pattern themselves. Also they had a system of naming which documented the lineage for all of the children through the father's side, not the mother's.

In dealing with the whites, the Senecas were

identified within the context of the nuclear family tradition familiar to white society. The Indians, at a loss for a surname, often resorted to the expediency of taking a name they had heard some white person called, especially one they admired.

> Juding by the frequent names of Jemison and Pierce we cannot make a correct estimate of descent, as when the Indians were first enrolled and must give an English name, many chose the name of some person admired for real worth.[19]

Parker notes that while the Seneca kept their hereditary names, because of commercial relations with the whites they began to adopt European names from various sources.[20] This was the beginning of a duality of family status that the Indians have had to contend with to present day.

Peter Crouse, with his nuclear family background from white society, established his own family in the same fashion. All of his children were given Christian names and they carried the Crouse surname of their father. In the Indian tradition, it was recognized that their mother, Chippany, was of the deer clan but the Crouse geneology was carried through to today. Reverend Alden was quite impressed with Peter's family. "His aquaw is a well-behaved, neat, and industrious woman and they have a numerous family of fine looking children.[21]

Many descendants of Peter Crouse are living on the Seneca Reservation today. They are proud of their ancester and are pleased to talk about him to interested listeners. Some have accumulated materials such as newspaper clippings and copies of the skit which was put on at the time of the big Crouse reunion in 1911.

Dema Crouse Stoffer is a good example of an interested Crouse descendant. She is the daughter of Sylvester Crouse, the son of Silas Crouse, who was the son of George, who was the son of Peter Crouse. That makes the captive her great, great, grandfather.[22]

Her recollection of Peter Crouse's family appears to be the same as in the Trippe manuscript.

> William had no children. George W. Crouse had seven children" Delilah, Silas, Sylvester, William, Bela, Alonzo, Lucy. Eldest child of George W. Crouse, Delilah Crouse married Guy Jamison and their children were Polly, Robert, Mary, Delia, Allan, Adam, Charles, Nathaniel, and Nelson. Silas Crouse, eldest grandson of the captive, and eldest son of George W. Crouse married Betsey Patterson. Their children were Emely, Susanna, Jonas, Sylvester, Charles, Martin, Jerome, Rosa, and Frank. Emely Crouse married Horace Jamison. Their children were Lillie and Willett.
> Susanna Crouse married William Tallchief. Children Jannie and Flora.
> Jonas Crouse married Electa Redeye, Children; Lavina, Aaron, Marian, Florence, and Katherine.
> Sylvester Crouse married Melina Halftown, Children were Sophia, Lola, Edison, Dema, Elon, Bernice, Ernest, Clifford
> Jerome Crouse married Hannah Cooper. Children Evaline, Wilford, Alberta, Edith, Lavina.
> Rose Crouse married Howard Logan, Children Arline, Newton, Edna, and Francis.
> Charles Crouse married 1st. Eva Lewis Child Jannie; Hettie Jemison, Child Elsie.
> Martin Crouse married Carrie Armstrong, Children Harietta, Sarah, Nancy and William.

Frank Crouse married Helen Blackchief, Children Rosetta, Roland, and Elon.[23]

The pattern of the Seneca family was gradually altered more and more toward white orientation with some families cutting off clan identification and affiliation completely. Most of them are somewhat aware of their clan, while the traditionalists choose to identify with the clan as much as possible under present conditions. The shift from hereditary chiefs to elected ones further accentuated the decline in clan responsibility for all except those who still maintained a preference for old ways and identified with the Longhouse.

The decline in the power of the clan was accompanied by an impetus to keep the women at home, rather than fieldwork or gathering, and have them busily engaged in those tasks which occupied white women's time. The Quaker Mission to the Senecas stressed this aspect. The Seneca woman being assured that this was the route which would cause the Creator to love them and bring them many good things.[24]

In his diary, Joseph S. Elkington, noted that change was taking place even though the Indians were not adapting rapidly to the new methods. . . .the Indians were slow in adopting improved modes of performing labour but some progress was manifest amongst them . . . the Indian women taught to spin. . .also to weave. . ."[25]

Despite the change of locale as to where some Seneca women worked and an apparent decline in the importance of the clan, the political power of the women remained very strong. Political office was still a male perogative but negotiations regarding the filling of these offices remained in the grasp of influential women on the reservation. In one instance, a female leader on the reservation found herself made a mother of the governor of Pennsylvania.

> Alice White. . .For many years she was the leader among the women at Coldspring. When the Cornplanter Indians were persuaded to put on an adoption ceremony for Governor Arthur H. James of Pennsylvania August 24, 1940, they induced her to go down and act as his mother.[26]

The art of medicine and healing among the Senecas was affected by the emergence of white science-oriented medicine, among the whites at first, and then competing with the traditional herbalists and curers of the reservation later.

Here we see the classic confrontation of personal, subjective intuitive-oriented medicine with the more impersonal, objective, clinically-oriented practice of healing. There continues to be an uneasy truce between them today.

Senecas are still very knowledgeable about plants and herbs for medicinal purposes and usually resort to these home remedies at the onset of illness. Ardent supporters of traditional medicine make great claims for cures brought about through this method but their numbers are greatly diminished.

Local doctors from white society are not as likely to be impressed. They are inclined to view the home remedies as sufficient for minor problems but would be skeptical of Indian medication for serious illness. When told of the marvelous recovery of one patient who had resorted to a special brew cooked up by a local herbalist, a surgeon from the area exclaimed. "He didn't look cured the last time I saw him!" The Indian had been brought into his office the previous week in very bad condition necessitating amputation of a limb. Hence the feeling on the part of the surgeon that often native medicine delays attention by competent medical practitioners.[27]

The two belief systems of medicine and healing continue to exist side-by-side without the one fully trusting the other. There has been some softening of attitudes with native healers being impressed by the feats of the white man's wonder drugs and skillful operations, and with white doctors showing more interest and sympathy with herbal medication and psychosomatic curing.

Of the many things brought over by the Europeans, none has had greater impact on the Indians than Christianity. The old gods and the Indians have never been the same since the "black robes" of the Jesuits and the fiery evangelists beat their way through the wilderness to minister the gospel to the red man.

The Jesuits had been in the forefront of French exploration and colonization. A remarkable number had reached the shores of North America to preach the gospel and convert the Indians to Christianity.

Seneca contact with the Jesuits had been somewhat limited due to geography and historical development. The French had been heavily involved with eastern Algonkian tribes and with the Hurons of the upper Great Lakes area. These being traditional enemies, the Senecas were not too disposed to become religiously involved. There was some contact with the black fathers; as early as 1657 they reached the Seneca towns in the area of the Genesee[28] but the influence was not so great as it was on the more easterly Iroquois such as the Mohawks.

The Senecas do show some Jesuit influence on their native religion in some aspects as confession of sins (which is done publicly) and venerating of some religious symbols such as the cross and rosary beads. On the non-religious side Jesuits introduced need food items among which was the apple.

. . .early introduced at Detroit, apple

> trees, (or seeds) from the province of Normandy. . .Those found in the vicinity of Geneva, Canandaigua, Honeoye Flats, and upon the Genesee River, were either propagated from them, or from seeds given the Seneca Indians by the Jesuit missionaries.[29]

The English colonists on the Atlantic Coast soon demonstrated a strong prejudice against the Indian way of life and saw their religious duty as one of conversion or annihilation. The strict Protestantism of the colonists brooked no nonsense in terms of faith and morals.

> . . .Although the Pope declared as far back as 1512 that the natives of America were descended from Adam and Eve, in colonial New England Cotton Mather thought that 'probably the Devil decoyed (them) hither in hopes that the gospel of the Lord Jesus Christ would never come here to destroy or disturb his absolute empire over them' As God's elected agents. . . the colonists must convert these 'tawny serpents' or annihilate them.[30]

The way the colonists on the east coast saw it, there could be no two-way exchange in the meeting of Indian and white culture. It had to be one way since they believed the white way superior. In regard to those few whites, such as Peter Crouse who became white Indians, it amounted to a strange and shocking development in the Puritan mind.[31] Indianization appeared to run counter to Christianization.

The Quakers of Philadelphia, themselves the object of scorn and persecution in some of the colonies, made a long and consistent effort to help the Indians. Their mission to the Senecas in the last decade of the eighteenth century was a model in judicious technical aid for people of a different culture. Fenton feels it was the Quakers of Philadelphia who invented the term technical assistance.[32]

> . . .educational and missionary work really started in 1798 with the arrival of three young Quakers from Philadelphia. . .Joel Swayne and Halliday Jackson settled down at Old Town, some nine or ten miles above Jessesadaga, where they planned to turn warriors into farmers and artisans. Henry Simmons, Jr. stayed with Cornplanter and took over the departments of morals and education. . .tried to make the Indians domestic, sober, and industrious by precept and example.[33]

After a few years, the Quakers decided they should move their operation off Indian reservation land so as not to appear intruding or taking away from the Indians what was rightfully theirs. They purchased some land from the Holland Land Company at a place on the east side of the river which was called Tunessassa.

> The Quakers built mills and introduced fences and farm implements. About 1806 they acquired from the Holland Land Company a tract near Quaker Bridge, New York, where they built a school for training 'in the useful arts.'[34]

The Quaker School was of great importance for the survival of the Senecas on the Allegany Reservation. It continued as an agency for peaceful social change and adjustment for a century and more until it was declared sub-standard and replaced by public schools of the State of New York. During the many years of existence, there were hundreds upon hundreds of young Indians educated there but very few converts. The Quakers did not believe in impulsive conversions.

The records testify that many Seneca

applied for admittance into the Society of Friends, but were rejected with regrets--standards for acceptance into the Quaker faith were far more stringent than the competing Christian religions.[35]

Despite the many assurances by the Quakers that they were after no pay or land for their efforts, some Senecas remained skeptical and fearful that there would be some demand made later on. It seemed incredible to some that whites would be doing all that and not expect the Indian to pay later on. In 1820, Thomas Stewardson received a letter from a chief of the Senecas asking the Quakers to "send a speech upon parchment stating in very positive terms that they will never take any of our land or money."[36]

Not all of the Senecas were inclined to follow the good example set by the visiting Quakers from Philadelphia. Chief Cornplanter told Jackson that there were men "of sobriety" among his people who wished to do the good things they were being shown to do but there were some who would not hear their words.[37]

There is evidence that Peter Crouse was one of those who heeded the good message and strove to follow the agricultural example set by the farming Quakers at Tunessassa. Other writers have borne out the report of Reverend Alden that the former captive was comfortably settled in a nice home amidst many well-tilled acres.

Not very much detail is given about Peter Crouse in the Quaker reports other than his presence and well-being. Although they may have had some reservations about his Indianization, there apparently was some visiting with him. Halliday Jackson reported that after one meeting with Chief Cornplanter and "assembled Indians" they went to his house. "And after these sayings were ended the Chiefs and Rulers of the people went a part unto the house of Peter* (footnote*A white captive.[38]

A number of questions were posed to the Quakers during discussion periods between the Senecas and their Christian teachers. Henry Simmons reported in his diary that on one occasion he was asked whether it was right for Indians and whites to mix in marriage. "I told them it was a bad question" notes Simmons, "it might be right for some but not for me."[39]

Another question was whether Indians and white people went together to the same place after death. "I told them there was but two places, a place for the Good, and a place for the Bad, of all Nations of People.[40]

The impact of the Quaker mission to the Senecas was one of two major efforts to show a good example and demonstrate the values of white Christian society. The committee for betterment of the Indians continues to this day.[41]

The second major effort to help the Senecas came through Protestant missionaries sent by the American Board of Commissioners for Foreigh Missions from Boston. Where the Friends mission had concentrated on the Seneca reservation at Allegany the Boston-based group concentrated on the Buffalo Creek areas.

> The first visit of a Protest missionary to the region of Buffalo Creek. . . was that of Rev. Samuel Kirkland, in the summer of 1788. . .(to) furnish to the Board of Commissioners in Boston, a particular account of the situation and numbers of the Senecas, their disposition toward the Christian religion, the prospects of usefulness to a missionary residing among them.[43]

Seneca response was cordial but not overly enthusiastic to this first emissary from the Protestant foreign mission from Boston. One white observer commented that "they preferred an Episcopal or Roman Catholic" who would baptize their children without any evidence of personal regeneration in the parents."[44]

For a time, after Kirkland's visit, there was little done in the way of Protestant Missionary work from Boston--for the Senecas in western New York. Thirty-eight years later in 1826, interest was rekindled when an organizational change in Protestant foreign mission work took place.

> In 1826-27 the United Foreign Missionary Society, an organization formed some years before by the Presbyterians, together with the Dutch and Associated Reformed churches, to conduct missionary work among the Indians of North and South America, transferred to the American Board the care of its Indian missions. . . (including) various New York tribes in the general region of Buffalo.[45]

The American Board responded enthusiastically to its new mandate and sought to extend the Protestant Mission from the Buffalo Creek area to Cattaraugus and Allegany. The year 1830 saw the Allegany Reservation Church organized. A resurgence of interest in 1831 and in 1932 Reverend Asher Bliss took charge of both the Cattaraugus and Allegany churches.[46]

Reverend Bliss reported, however, that the revival of religious interest was not confined to a Christian resurgence alone.

> The pagan portion of the two Reservations availed themselves of the opportunity to build up and strengthen their cause against Christianity. Dances were multiplied, old ceremonies revived, and great effort was put forth to add interest and eclat to all their proceedings.[47]

In a letter to H. R. Schoolcraft in 1845, Reverend Bliss spoke of the reversion of some of the baptized Indians. Declaring that it was to be expected from "converts out of heathenish darkness," he placed the number of defectors from Christianity as "not probably more than one in ten."[48]

Protestant missionary work among the Senecas was tremendously furthered by someone who, in the words of Fenton, was one of the really great men of his day. Together with his wife, Reverend Asher Wright devoted a lifetime of service to the Indians. It is indeed "one of the finest chapters in Seneca history."[49]

Asher Wright, ordained in 1831, went to the Seneca Reservation at Buffalo Creek the same year and remained in the service of the Seneca until his death in 1875. He and his wife Laura learned the Seneca language so well they could not only speak it fluently but also constructed teaching materials for instruction in the language.[50]

In his preaching the gospel to the Senecas and trying to improve their condition, Asher Wright was aided immensely by the untiring efforts of his wife. Not only did Laura Wright give him invaluable assistance in his church work but she also took greatly to heart the welfare of the poor and the orphans.

> In 1847 a disastrous epidemic of typhoid struck and Mrs. Wright found many Senecas in need of help. When Laura Wright took in the orphans of this epidemic she honored an ancient virtue of the Seneca people which they immediately sensed and supported, enabling her to walk with confidence into the homes of Christian and pagan alike.[51]

A number of years before, in 1854, Mrs. Wright had taken in some orphan children when an Indian had died leaving a large number of children with no one to look after them. With the help of a Quaker from Baltimore named Philip E. Thomas the Thomas Indian School had its beginning. A cooperative effort between protestant Board and Quakers brought about this school and asylum for destitute Indian children which would serve them well for over a century.

We don't know if Peter Crouse was ever in contact with Reverend and Mrs. Wright but we do know that two other white captives became strongly attached to this missionary couple.

Old White Chief, who had been captured as a little boy along the Susquehanna, became very attached to Reverend Wright. It was to him that Old White Chief told the details of his capture and subsequent life among the Indians.[52]

Mary Jemison was another white captive who became very attached to the Wrights. One day Mrs. Wright was called to the bedside of the aged white woman who was upset because she had promised her mother when they were captured that she would say a prayer every day so she would't forget she was a Christian. Unfortunately, Mary had forgotten to do this and now couldn't even remember how the prayer went.

> Mrs. Wright gave the Lord's Prayer slowly and then it was evident a chord had been touched and she immediately became convulsed with weeping and said 'That is the Prayer my mother taught me.'[53]

The Presbyterians, who had been the moving force at the time of the organization of the United Foreign Missionary Society in 1826, withdrew from the Board in 1870. Upon this withdrawal, the Seneca Mission was given entirely to their care.[54]

The Presbyterian Church remains strong and active on the Allegany Reservation to this day. Reverend M. F. Trippe served as missionary-in-charge at the Presbyterian Church at Jimersontown for many years,[55] and his wife's manuscript on the

Crouse family is one of the best sources of information regarding the captive and his descendants.

The descendants of Peter Crouse have been strongly Christian throughout the years. His childhood background had undoubtedly given him some background in Christianity and Reverend Alden furnishes us with a very clear personal account of the captive's receptivity to further instruction in the Bible.

> He thankfully received one of the Bibles, of which we had brought a number from the Meadville Bible Society for gratuitous distribution. He has never been taught to read; yet his children are learning, and he expressed the hope of one day profiting, through their aid, by the contents of this sacred volume.[56]

The wife of Peter Crouse, Chippany (Christian name-Rachel) was known to be strong in her faith. Also it is believed her mother was driven from her original home in Onondaga on the charges of being a witch when actually it was because she was a Christian.[57] On the Mission Church rolls for 1848 there is listed "Old Mrs. Crouse" which was probably Chippany.

Several of Peter's descendants have been identified as being especially strong in their Christian faith and exercised leadership in the community.

George W. Crouse, second son of Peter Crouse and first child of the marriage with Chippany, is listed as Deacon on the rolls of the Allegany Mission Church for 1855.

> Mrs. Alfred L. Jemison remembers with pleasure visits at the home of her grandfather George W. Crouse. . .He and Deacon Levi Halftown were very

> close friends and worked together as farmers and in all the interests of the church.[59]

Also listed on the church rolls for 1855 were Peter T. Crouse, son of the captive, Silas Crouse son of George W. and eldest grandson of Peter the captive; Miss Lucy Crouse, daughter of George W.; Mrs. Betsey Crouse, Mrs. George Crouse, Mrs. John Crouse, and "Old Mrs. Crouse" with the notation that she died January 1, 1859.[60]

Silas Crouse was a very zealous Christian, following his deacon-father's good example he took an active part in church affairs. For many years he was the only professing Christian between Quaker Bridge and Red House, New York.[61]

Mrs. Trippe mentions that when in 1882 her husband Reverend M. F. Trippe made his visits to the reservation, the home of Silas Crouse was to him "a haven of rest and hours of God" with the services attended by Silas' family of eleven persons and by the family of his sister Emily Jemison. Later his sons were active in getting a church for Cold Spring, New York.

> In 1905 the sons of Silas Crouse took a leading part in securing a church at Cold Spring, purchasing the school house where the youth of that section had been trained. It was remodeled into a pretty little church and standing on a hill facing the Crouse homes speaks in memory of them.[62]

One of Silas Crouse's sons names Jonas is mentioned by Congdon as having very strong Christian preference, with little sympathy for the Indian beliefs. In an incident several decades later, he showed his geniality and generosity and, Congdon feels, lack of concern for the Indian status.

During the New Year's celebration

> January 23, 1937 they had an adoption ceremony and Jonas Crouse offered to give his own name to the candidate and get a new one for himself. He was as faithful a Christian as anyone and did not have much use for an Indian name.[63]

The Christian tradition remains strong among the Crouses and for a large number of Senecas on the Reservations. The great prestige of Chief Cornplanter had imparted to the Quaker effort the force of local support at both Cornplanter's village, Jenushadaga, and at Cold Spring. The old chief was to change his mind later on but it was he who brought the needs of the Senecas at Allegany to the attention of the Quakers.

> . . .as early as 1791, his confidence won by the friendliness of the Quakers whom he had met while on a visit to Philadelphia, Cornplanter had proposed that they take two Seneca boys to educate. This request turned the attention of the Quakers particularly to the Senecas.[64]

Interest remained high at Allegany for the Quaker experiment and the gospel of the whites. The missionary Jabez B. Hyde reported in 1811 that support for Christianity at the Allegany Reservation continued to be widely demonstrated. "The Allegany Chiefs (except one) respresenting a population of more than 550 souls, declared in favor of the Gospel and espoused the cause of the Christian party."[65]

Some critics of the missionary activity of the time have felt that the churchmen were misled by the reaction of the Indians to their preachings. This criticism holds that the Indians were merely being polite and they "neither believed nor understood that to which they had so promptly assented."[66]

An important indicator of the validity of the religious conversion among a people is the ability or lack of ability to attract native clergy. One native clergyman, well-trained and enthusiastic about the new religion, is worth thousands of converts. A good example of this among the Senecas was that of Alfred Halftown.

> 'We have a new preacher at Allegany, Alfred Halftown! He is a good preacher. He gets up at five and walks 25 miles to Jeminson town and preaches at eleven. There he has dinner at Will Hoag's. After dinner he walks back to Cold Spring and preaches there, he holds a meeting at Old Town at 5 o'clock. After that he sometimes stays overnight but if his work at home needs him he goes on home that night.' Mr. Pierce added with enthusiasm" 'Oh, he's a good preacher!'[67]

It was not all smooth going for Christianity on the Seneca Reservation. Some of the Indians resented the progress made by this new religion and also they saw many contradictions between what the white man said in his religion and how he behaved.

Many years before Lincoln's Emancipation Proclamation, some Senecas had been in contact with white slaveholders and had been repulsed by the sight of human beings held in this type of bondage In 1803, a Chief at Allegany, wishing to find out what kind of people these emissaries from Philadelphia were, asked very directly of them:

> 'Do the Quakers keep any slaves?' He was answered in the negative. He said he was very glad to hear it; for if they did, he could not think so well of them as he now did--that he had been at the city of Washington last winter, on business of the nation, and found that many white people kept blacks in slavery, and used them no better than horses.[68]

The great sachem Red Jacket remained throughout his lifetime opposed to Christianity. He used his high intelligence, sharp wit, and oratorical skills to annoy the white preachers, and their Christian adherents. In a famous speech Red Jacket asked a mocking rhetorical question worthy of a Voltaire. "Brother, you say there is but one way to worship and serve the Great Spirit; if there is but one religion, why do you white people differ so much about it? Why not all agree, as you can all read the book?"[69]

Where the Quakers from Philadelphia tried their best to answer the questions asked of them by these careful thinkers and powerful orators of the forest, there were others who were not so patient. When Red Jacket concluded his speech by saying that if the Creator has made us all so different then can it not be assumed He meant us to have different religions, the missionary became upset and refused further discussion.

> The chiefs and others then drew near the missionary to take him by the hand, but he would not receive them, and hastily rising from his seat said 'that there was no fellowship between the religion of God and the works of the devil, and therefore could not join hands with them.' Upon this being interpreted to them 'they smiled, and retired in a peaceable manner.[70]

Until his death in 1830, Red Jacket used his tremendous powers of oratory against the Christian religion. A hard-drinking man, he was opposed to all change whether those of Handsome Lake or Cornplanter and his Quaker friends.[71]

Blacksnake added his voice to those clamoring against Christianity. Like Red Jacket, he saw a distinction between the Indian and the white man with Christianity meant for the whites. Blacksnake declared that the mission of the Saviour was to the white and not to the Indian, it being merely an innovation for the Indians.[72]

Seneca reaction against Christianity was more pronounced on some of the other reservations. Where Jabez Hyde had reported encouraging news from Allegany in 1811, the news was discouraging farther north. The Senecas at Cattaraugus, Tonowanda, and Genesee, with a population of about 1,000, "stood steadfast in their opposition."[73]

Perhaps the worst blow of all against Christianity among the New York Senecas was the change of heart of the leading chief at Allegany. Chief Cornplanter, whose idea it was originally to invite the Quakers in, had what Turner called a "relapse into paganism."[74] The man whom Kirkland had been so pleased to convert to the Christian religion in 1790 in Philadelphia had changed his mind. So much so that in a council meeting in 1821 he emphatically told the Quakers: "I am authorized by the Great Spirit to tell you that you must take your liberty, and move off from the Cold Spring, and attend to your own business, and the ministry, and all other people must do so too . . ."[75]

Cornplanter's break with Christianity was complete and irrevocable by 1833. At a meeting that year he declared he had tried it but could not continue and did not wish to have anything more to do with that religion.

> It is useless to attempt to teach us Christianity for even though our bodies may be present at your meetings, our spirits are entirely given up to our old religion. . .the old chief made all those who had listened to the committee at all confess their sins publicly and swear renewed allegiance to paganism and that they would never again attend a christian meeting.[76]

Closely tied to Christianity was another

trait which the whites introduced to the Senecas and which was to have an impact on their culture. This was the art of writing.

The Senecas, like many other pre-literate people, were quite fascinated by the white man's writing. They had relied for many years on an associational system where certain marks or pictures stood for something which the "reader" would then recall and give the message from the wampum belt or a stick. Script or linear writing was unknown to them prior to their contact with white society.

Literacy is the mark of civilization, according to Fenton, and the printed page became the new wampum.[77] The Senecas, who may have felt they already were civilized enough, were both appreciative and apprehensive about the power of writing.

Red Jacket was properly appreciative of what writing could do for someone in his day and age. When told that Colonel Pickering, whom Red Jacket had bested severely in the treat-making at Newtown in 1791, had been promoted from Postmaster General to Secretary of War, he told Thomas Morris "Ah, we began our public career about the same time; he knew how to read and write, I did not and he has got ahead of me, but if I had known how to read and write, I would have been ahead of him"[78]

Some of the Senecas were distrustful of this power of the whites. It appeared to have a potentially bad influence on their young people as was pointed out at Lancaster in 1774. The Indian orator, speaking for the Five Nations, turned down an invitation to send Indian youths to the white man's colleges.

> We are convinced you mean to do us good by your proposal, and we thank you heartily. . .different nations have different conceptions of things. . . our ideas of this kind of education happen not to be the same as yours . .

> several of our people were . . . instructed in all your sciences; but when they came back to us, they were bad runners, ignorant of every means of living in the woods; unable to bear either cold or hunger; they neither knew how to build a cabin, take a deer or kill an enemy; spoke a language imperfectly, were therefore neither fit for hunters, warriors or counsellers; they were totally good for nothing.[79]

The experience of the Seneca called Farmer's Brother echoed the fears of the Indian speaker at Lancaster. One of Farmer's Brother's grandsons had decided to go to college at Philadelphia. After he had be gone for a time, the grandfather decided to pay him a visit. The boy was not at home but he was directed to where the grandson was expected to be. Each time he kept missing him and by the time he caught up with him, Farmer's Brother had been in a tavern, a gambling den, a brothel, and a dance hall.[80]

Apparently the acquired habits from college carried over to the detriment of some students when they returned to the reservation. In one issue of a Quaker Journal, it is noted:

> . . .the natives being much prejudiced against their children receiving literary instruction; owing in great measure to the bad conduct of one of their people on his return home (son of a principal chief) that had been educated amongst the whites.[81]

It was very evident to such men as Chief Cornplanter that the old way of life, although it might have been the preferred one for the Senecas, was no longer a realistic possibility. Although the older people could manage to get through somehow, he was farsighted in his concern for the coming generations. Being a religious man, he concluded it was the wish of the Great Spirit that the Seneca must change their way of life.[82]

Once having decided that the Senecas would have to take this great step, he looked around for the best teachers to help his people learn the ways of the whites. The Quakers of Philadelphia were a good choice as they were a capable and prosperous people who had earned the trust of the Indians. In a letter sent to the Society of Friends at Philadelphia in 1791, Cornplanter made clear the high regard he had of them "Your fathers dealt honestly with our fathers, and they have engaged us to remember it: we wish our children to be taught the same principles by which your fathers were guided."[83]

The arrival of three young men from Philadelphia signaled the beginning of the Quaker mission to the Senecas on the Allegany. It was in the year 1798 that Joel Swayne, Halliday Jackson, and Henry Simmons, Jr. began their labors on behalf of Cornplanter's people at Jenushadaga (Burnt House) and at Old Town about nine miles upriver.

Henry Simmons, Jr. was given the task of teaching the Seneca children and he set up a school in Cornplanter's house.[84]

Not surprisingly, since several families lived at Cornplanter's, Simmons turned his efforts toward better facilities and in a letter to the Quaker Committee on Indian Affairs in 1799 reported that "a commodious school house" had been built with the help of the Indians.[85]

Halliday Jackson made note of this important event by recollecting:

> One of the Friends opened a school at Cornplanter's village, and remained there through the winter. At times nearly twenty children attended, and

> made some progress in learning to spell and read. . .they were very irregular in their attendance, and no great progress in learning was made.[86]

When the Quakers moved off the Allegany Reservation in 1806, they built another school at Tunessassa to train the Indians in the "useful arts." This school was still in existence as late as 1941.[87]

At the school in Cornplanter's town (Jenushadaga), there was a veritable parade of schoolmasters. In 1814 Robert Clendenon and his wife and daughter were the teachers. In 1815 the Western Missionary Society sent Samuel Oldham, then Joseph Elkinton in 1816.

> . . . school was an off-and-on affair usually reflecting cycles of Indian attraction and aversion to white ways, as when Cornplanter himself in February 1821 ordered Elkinton to close his school and go home. This mirrored the strong feeling aroused by the Indian land swindles of that era.[88]

In a Quaker report on the status of the Indian schools, it was pointed out that attendance by the Indian children was irregular but it was felt this was due to 'various causes, chiefly, perhaps, to their being detained at home to work. . . .[89] Whether the Quakers were unaware of Indian resentments concerning land swindles, didn't feel that it influenced school attendance, or just did not want to mention it, is unknown.

That a resentment against schools and the white man's reading and writing existed is undoubtedly true. Their chief had asked for it so the feeling against it was not out in the open but smoldering underneath and especially evident as Cornplanter got older and less sure of himself.

> (some) . . .of them had become opposed to their children's being instructed in school learning, giving this as a reason 'that they were more lieable to be corrupted by bad white people.'[90]

By 1820 opposition to schooling had become quite strong by some Indians, although others favored retention. Cornplanter was going through one of his negative periods towards whites and this gave those opposed to reading and writing greater weight.

One Indian told Elkinton he should not try to teach the children after having been forbidden by the Council to do so. He also gave the school teacher some additional bad news. "He told me that several of the Indians felt very little satisfaction in their children having attended school so long, without learning anything of account.[91]

The situation degenerated further for the harassed school teacher when he was visited by three chiefs who warned him about going on their land to teach school. There had also been threats to smash the small boat he used to cross the river from Tunessassa to Cold Spring. One Indian threatened to hit him with a stick.[92] Apparently, there would be no official help forthcoming from the state or U. S. Government as Indian Agent Chapin wrote a letter telling how sorry he was that the "Pagan Party" opposed the school and adding that he had no funds to offer to keep it going.[93]

As so often happens when quarrels arise about schools, the children are forgotten, pushed to one side and unheard. Very Basic, but not very much explored, was the question of educational value for the children. Were they able to profit from the schooling experience?

In a letter from one of the teachers, Reverend William Hall to H. R. Schoolcraft there is a very favorable evaluation of the Indian children. "Those who attend regularly, evince a capacity to acquire knowledge, equalling the whites, and one of our schools will suffer nothing in comparison with common country schools."[94]

Hall's evaluation of the worth of Indian schoolchildren is the same as that of Reverend Asher Bliss. In his letter to H. R. Schoolcraft in 1845, one hundred and nine years before the Supreme Court school decision in Brown vs Topeka, Bliss said there was no essential difference between them and white children.

> The fact that Indian children usually make slow progress in studying English books can be accounted for in three ways: They generally have little or no assistance from their parents at home 2. They are irregular in their attendance for want of order and discipline on the part of the parents. 3. Being ignorant of the English language, it is a long time before they comprehend fully the instruction of their teachers.[95]

Bliss went on to say that these factors make school a dull and uninteresting place for both pupils and teacher but that "when they can once rise above these circumstances, and overcome these obstacles, they make good proficiency in their studies.[96]

The coming of the scools and the arguments pro and con all took place while the captive Peter Crouse was living at the Allegany Reservation. He had been captured twenty years before the coming of the Quakers and indeed was in the same building Cornplanter's home when Simmons began the very first schooling there. There is no doubt which side Peter Crouse was on in the controversy over reading and writing. Reverend Alden had mentioned that when he visited Peter Crouse in 1816, Peter could not read but his children were learning.[97]

Peter's children may have been at the Cold Spring School which Alden said consisted of seventeen Indian boys diligently instructed by Joseph Elkinton at the expense of the Society of Friends, in Philadelphia.[98]

Letters from Tunessassa dated December 20, 1837 and January 18, 1838, from Joseph and Rebecca Battey to the Quaker committee on Indians give a strong testimonial to the scholastic efforts of the son of Peter Crouse, also named Peter. In the 1838 letter it is interesting to note the statement: ". . .the natives have a school at Old Town taught by Peter Crouse a native he gives good attention to his business several of his scholars are learning to write and two of them study arithmetic.[99]

Where Peter's son is referred to as "a native" in the 1838 letter, Joseph Battey writing a letter of December 6, 1840 refers to "Peter T. Crouse, a half-blood Indian, teaches at a school one mile from the Council House at Cold Spring."[100] Either way, native or half-blood, we do have evidence that the Crouses believed in the value of an education.

The expertise of Peter T. Crouse's use of the written word is demonstrated in one of his letters written July 27, 1850. The letter was in reply to the Historian Draper's letter of April 23, 1850, requesting some specific information about the Seneca Indians.

The Crouse letter answers Draper's questions, point by point, and then is signed P. T. Crouse with a flourish! The letter not only shows that the captive's son knew how to write well but it also shows an excellent mastery of Seneca history.[101]

Eventually, the battle pro and con writing was resolved in favor of the "White man's wampum." That some Senecas never reconciled their opposition is undoubtedly true, but each succeeding generation felt more and more pressure to learn and more and more good reason to master the written art.

Small, one-room schools on the Reservation gave way to the complex educational facilities in the centralized school districts of New York State It was soon recognized that elementary and even high school education was not enough and that Senecas should be encouraged into higher education

The Seneca Nation Educational Foundation, with headquarters in Salamanca, New York, is evidence of the Seneca concern for higher education. With a full-time director, it works closely with students in the public schools of Salamanca, Gowanda, and Silver Creek districts. In 1972 this involved 900 students, with 70% of those graduating that year going on to post-secondary schools.[102]

Just as the eighteenth century was about to come to a close, in a crude cabin near the Allegany River on the Cornplanter grant, the life of a man appeared also to be at an end. The half-brother of Cornplanter lay motionless on a bed. He seemed dead to those who looked in on him. Blacksnake said later that he went into the cabin to see the body and it was as cold as death.[103]

The man on the cot was Ga-ne-o-di-yo (Handsome Lake) and he did not pass away during that illness. Rather, he came to consciousness and announced to relatives and friends that though he had been briefly in the next world, he was coming back to this world to help his people in their time of crisis.

> He said he was going to get well again--that during his trance, he had seen three angels who told him he would recover, and what medicines he must use. . . that accomplished he was to devote himself for the good of his people. That he must

> convene them together and tell them they must stop drinking ardent spirits as it was a great evil, and would, if continued to be indulged in, prove their destruction. The angels told him that he should have great power to heal the sick . . . that he must go among the Six Nations and preach to them for their reformation.[104]

This marked the beginning of the Code of Handsome Lake. The sick man did just as he said the angels told him to do. He got up from his sick bed and although a heavy drinker before, he refrained from the "drink of the white man." This took place about June 15, 1799, and Handsome Lake spent the rest of his life preaching sobriety, gainful employment, and good family relations. After about 14 years of preaching, he died in 1815. His work did not die with him; today there is a determined group of followers who continue to honor his memory and his teachings.

In his pronouncements, Handsome Lake showed a great deal of influence from Christian sources. Simmons had been teaching school at Cornplanter's house at the time of Handsome Lake's illness and it is quite possible that the biblical stories he told the Indian children were of interest to the man lying sick on a cot nearby.[105]

The Quakers were not particularly pleased with the Prophet's emphasis on keeping the old festivals and dances. To them this seemed a sliding back to what they viewed as pagan worship. However, they could not criticize the message of Handsome Lake's religion as it was not very different from the things they had been telling the Senecas, regarding temperance, work, and morals. "Simmons himself recognized that Handsome Lake's teachings were aimed at the same mark as his but their unorthodox and strongly red coloring disturbed him."[106]

What was disturbing to the Quakers, and to

others, also, was the stress Handsome Lake put on continuing the old ceremonies and his rejection of the white man's reading, writing, and Christianity It did not seem like progress toward the goals the Quakers had in mind. They did not recognize the possibility that Handsome Lake was bringing the Christian message to the Indians in a form that was much better understood and received by those Senecas who wished to remain traditionalists.

While Handsome Lake was out of this world and was being conducted through the next world, he was shown some interesting things such as a chief wheeling dirt to atone for his sin of selling reservation land. Most dramatically he saw his dead son and the dead daughter of Cornplanter.

There was an aspect of introspection which the Quakers should have appreciated in that the angel who was his guide pointed out Handsome Lake's failings.

> He then told me of my failing which was that of getting drunk some time back, but as I had declined that practice and concluded if I got well to do so no more they would forgive me and I must also quit all kinds of frolicking and dancing except the worship dance for that was right as we did not make use of any Spirits at that time. . . (Indians) must not drink whiskey for that belonged to white people and was not made for Indians.[107]

In their disapproval of that which was not Christian, the Quakers (as well as other missionaries) viewed the emergence of the religion of Handsome Lake's followers as paganism and the group as the "Pagan Party." This helped polarize the factions on the reservations as politics became part of the identification of the two groups.

With its emphasis on traditionalism, the followers of the Code of Handsome Lake became very strongly opposed to any additional land sales. The Indian agent Chapin wrote a letter to Dearborn in 1802 bemoaning the lack of progress in closing a land deal.

> I left Buffalo Creek three days ago - - - much pains was taken to bring the Indians to close the bargain for the mile strip of land on Niagara River but proved ineffectual. The principal objection was that the Great Spirit had lately appeared to Abeel's Brother (Cornplanter) and ordered that no more of their land must be sold.[108]

In commenting on life on the reservation today Fenton praised the effect which the Code of Handsome lake has on the Seneca communitry at Cold Spring, near where this all began.

> Life at Coldspring is a going concern and the longhouse settlement has a culture of its own. Albeit this culture is not the integrated culture of an aboriginal Seneca community, nevertheless faith in the revelation of the Seneca Prophet, Handsome Lake, unites a small autonomous group of families and gives them a sense of belonging to something which is ancient and respectable; and they cherish the last vestiges of that culture, which their somewhat isolated life on the reservation has engendered.[109]

The Seneca economic system was severely altered by the white man's intrustion into their area of dominance. The stable system of maize horticulture supplemented by hunter-gathering was prostrated by the trampling boots of white invaders.

Traditional concepts of land-holding by the Senecas were sorely tried by white concepts of land ownership. In this respect the system of communal ownership of the Senecas was ravaged by losses to the voracious land appetite of the Holland and the Ogden Land Companies, the shrinkage of tribal lands, and pressure to subdivide their remaining acreage into individual holdings. Their good friends the Quakers among others urged them to divide their lands into parcels for private ownership.

> The Quakers felt that the dividing of communal lands into individual family holdings, as practiced by the Whites would act as a civilizing factor. This sentiment was incorporated in one of the first messages brought by the early Quakers to the Allegany Seneca near the close of the eighteenth century.[110]

The Quakers interpreted any evidence of fencing on the part of the Indians as a step forward in the right direction. In a letter to the Committee on Indians in Philadelphia, dated June 16, 1799, Simmons, Swayne, and Jackson reported that "One Indian has fenced in a farm near ours; and more are about doing it. . .[111]

In order to praise the Indians and be sure they knew that this was the right direction, the Quakers addressed the Senecas in a council meeting:

> Brothers, we are pleased to see a quantity of new fence made this summer near where our young men live, and we would not have you get discouraged at the Labour it takes, for if you will clear a little more land every year, and fence it, you will soon get enough to raise what Bread you want, as well as some for Grass to make hay for Winter.[112]

Exactly twenty years after Sullivan said he had destroyed 60,000 bushels of corn in the Seneca lands near the Genesee and Broadhead reported destroying "crops of corn as fine as any he'd ever seen," on his punitive expedition to the upper Allegheny, whites were now complimenting Indians on their agricultural endeavors. They were assuring them that fencing is what made the difference!

Well into the nineteenth century, the Quakers could still report good tidings from Allegany. "About Old Town, there is a manifest change for the better (6/19/1847), both in the buildings, farming, and domestic economy. There is still however much room for advancement. . .[113]

A person with more interest and sympathy for native traditions, such as Reverend Asher Wright, could understand what a conflict it was for the Senecas to change to private, individually-owned land. Their claim to the land was through centuries of acquisition and land once in their domain belonged to all the Senecas and to the other nations of the confederacy as well.[114] "Fencing in of land was a radical shift in the idea of ownership and must have caused comment because a fence is the essence of exclusive ownership in private property."[115]

The intrusion of the whites on to the Seneca lands was not limited to land companies and covetous municipalities. Sometimes individuals simply helped themselves to property they wanted without any pretext of purchase or agreement. These people were simply squatting and in 1880, in a case taken to court by the Seneca Nation against John Crooks, Judge Loren L. Lewis said that "adverse possession was good against the Seneca Nation," and they have never been able to get the land back.[116]

The Seneca economic system was also modified in regard to the production of goods. As a stone age people before the coming of the whites, they had relied exclusively on hand labor. With the introduction of European and American trade goods there was pressure to move away from manual crafts to manufactured goods.

The superiority of the metal kettle, whether it was tin, copper, or brass was readily apparent over the traditional wooden containers, which obviously could not be put directly over the fire, thereby requiring the heating of stones before one could get hot water. Along with the gun and blanket, the kettle became a prime example of dependence on the whites for certain manufactured goods.

In order to fit into this system, the Indian had to acquire new skills (trades in the white viewpoint) or rely to a degree unknown in former times on the securing of forest products desired by the whites. The fur trade in North America was one of the results of this kind of pressure. Once the market for fur goods declined because of changing styles in Europe and America, the Indian was forced to go back to to subsistence farming and hunting. By the end of the nineteenth century wild game was extremely scarce in western New York and western Pennsylvania. Farming was not attractive for many Seneca males so they became laborers on the railroads, sawmills, lumber camps and eventually into structural steel.

Simmons and other Quakers had warned the Senecas that the day was coming when they no longer would be able to rely on hunting to provide their needs. Pickering addressed them on the same subject in a letter dated February 15, 1796.

> . . . You already know that game is becoming scarce, and have reason to expect that in a few years more it will be gone, what then will you do to feed and clothe yourselves, your wives and children.[117]

The scarcity of game and the great loss of territory made it necessary for the Senecas to modify their food production system. Crowded on small reservations, unable to bring in the large quantities of bear meat, venison, fish, and small game as in the past, the only alternatives were to work for the whites or to make the land more productive.

In making the land produce more, the old method of slash and burn and then plant with a dibble stick had to be changed. The white man's plough was the answer to the need for greater foodstuffs to be produced on less acreage.

> The plough was introduced instead of the hoe for preparing their fields for crops, and the men were induced to relieve the women from the laborious parts of husbandry, and a change was so far effected in public opinion amongst the natives, that they were not looked upon with disdain for so doing.[118]

Chief Cornplanter had seen this need to change from the old ways and had opened the way for his people to go from horticulture to agriculture. The agriculturalist depends on his plow to break the sod, turn it over, and then "fit" the land with drag or horrow. Much more care goes into preparation of a field as the stumps, and rocks cannot be left there the way the Indians were accustomed to doing. This kind of heavy work requires males in the fields and the help of draft animals for pulling and hauling.

The presence of farm livestock was an entirely new thing for the Senecas. They had not been a pastoral people and therefore had no experience with any domestic animal other than the dog. Unlike the dog, the draft animals were a threat to their crops if allowed to roam and hence the need for fences. Also unlike the dog, draft animals had to feed on hay and grain during the winter when no pasture was available. This made it necessary to plant fields for the support of livestock, something entirely new for the Senecas. With more and more fields to plant, additional ploughs and animals were critically needed. To help meet this need in 1802 the U.S. Government instructed the Indian agent Chapin to supply the

Senecas with some ploughs and farm animals.

> To such of the Chiefs of the Seneca Nation you can most confide in, you will deliver for the purposes above stated, two or three ploughs with an equal number of yoke of male, hardy oxen. . .three or four milch cows and twelve sheep.[119]

The reluctance of Seneca males to become farmers is best understood in terms of traditional values and male roles existing in that society before white intrusion. Not wishing to damage other people's opinion of them or their own self-image, Seneca males were unenthusiastic about farming as an occupation. Slowly, some change did take place. "As long as the people concentrated in settlements, the men could not be induced to farm, but with gradual acceptance of farming, families scattered on adjacent farmsteads.[120]

As early as 1801, the Quakers reported that a few Senecas were ploughing and becoming good farmers. Being skeptical of this new method, the Indians carried out experiments to check productivity of fields. Jackson felt there were a ten-fold increase in using the new way of agriculture over the old method of horticulture but the Senecas had to see for themselves. Their method of verification is startlingly modern demonstrating the keen intelligence which Senecas could bring to bear on a problem that interested them.

> They took a very cautious method of determining whether it was likely to be an advantageous change to them or not. Several parts of a large field were ploughed, and the intermediate spaces prepared by their women with the hoe, according to former custom. It was all planted with corn, and the parts ploughed produced much the heaviest crop; the stalks being more than

a foot higher, and proportionately stouter than those on the hoed ground.[121]

The Quakers continued to urge the Senecas toward the new agricultural way of life, and applauded their improvements in that direction. They especially praised the assistance males were giving women in tasks that previously were considered female work and also praised them for their building of better housing. To the Quakers this was evidence they were making progress toward the "habits of civilized life."[122]

Forced to modify their economic system to survive the onslaught of white invasion on all sides, the Senecas from their reservation areas could attempt to retain some vestige of their culture and remain aloof from the ever-present sea of American culture around them. It was virtually impossible, however, to keep entirely apart from white society. Over the years too many things had happened which bound them with the whites and many more events would continue to bring them together in the future.

Cornplanter, for example, would have much preferred to keep the Senecas to themselves after the tragic years of the American Revolutionary period. But he could not keep out the whites with their hunger for land and with those wonderful trade goods which the Indians desired so strongly. Ironically, Cornplanter himself had been a side effect of an economic venture in that his father was a Dutch peddler plying his wares from one Indian village to another.[123]

One of the hoped-for results from the Treaty of Fort Stanwix was that the Senecas, as well as the rest of the Iroquois nations, could remain "unto themselves" and in peaceful separateness. "General Henry Dearborn, the Secretary of War, . . .forbade all persons from disturbing the Indians 'in their quiet possession of said lands.'[124]

Events conspired not to make this quiet possession possible. The reservation lands, those tiny bits of former territory still remaining in the Seneca control, were being eroded by a tide of what Fenton has called "intemperance, bribery, infidelity, apathy, and bitter factionalism between Christians and Pagans.[125] "The impact came in January 1838 when realization dawned that some 114,869 acres had been sold for $1.75 per acre.[126]

Fortunately, the sale of Indian lands was finally stopped soon enough for the Senecas to have some acreage they could call their own. On these acres, approximately 40,000 acres at Allegany where Peter Crouse had once lived, life had its own pace. There is an easy and unhurried tempo. People are not madly rushing around; they have time to talk to each other and be neighborly

Deardorff mentions that once while visiting on the Allegany Reservation he noticed that the clock had not been changed from standard time to daylight saving time. When he mentioned this, an Indian woman said "What's the difference?" [127]

In 1845, two years before the death of Peter Crouse, the New York State Legislature enacted a law which was to have far-reaching effects on the political system of the Seneca. The political structure of the old League had been in shambles since the American Revolution and now the stage was set for a political rebirth of the Seneca nation.

> . . .the Legislature . . . the 8th of May 1845, passed a law defining their rights; granting them corporate privileges, legalizing certain offices on the elective principle.[128]

This enabling legislation came at just the right time for the Senecas. The scandalous land sales of the Buffalo Creek and western New York lands had lost to the Senecas all their remaining territory in New York State. This was a horrendous "seven years of trouble" for the Senecas; 1837-1845 and Reverend Asher Wright is credited with bringing about a compromise agreement which kept the Allegany and Cattaraugus Reservations for the Seneca Nation.[129]

> Wright was convinced. . .that the Treaty (to sell the remaining lands) had set back the cause of civilization. Of 2,422 Senecas he counted, only 145 had favored the treaty; and 2,277 had opposed it--certainly enough under the old system of unanimity, or even simple majority, to defeat it on referendum. Deprived by fraud and forsaken by . . . the Great White Father. . .the Senecas in 1845 abandoned the graves of their fathers and removed with Wright to Cattaraugus.[130]

With the help of the timely passage of the law of 1845 by the New York State Legislature, the Senecas took a truly revolutionary step. They "dehorned" or threw out of office the hereditary chiefs. That in itself was not revolutionary because the system had allowed for this in the past But in 1848 the Senecas did not proceed to fill the vacant positions by the time-honored method of kinship and clan mothers. Instead they adopted a constitution, incorporated under the new state law and proceeded to hold elections for the vacant offices. In the same year of the great revolutions in Europe, an aboriginal people of North America effected one of their own.

> The old government by chiefs had served well as long as the elected officials conducted themselves with honesty and dignity. The corruption of these chiefs and their inability to prevent further loss of lands was all too evident at Buffalo Creek.[131]

Corrupted chiefs does not explain it alone.

They could have been replaced and that would have served as a strong warning to the new ones coming to office. The Senecas went beyond this; they threw out the whole system of hereditary chiefs and clan control. This would indicate a complete disillusionment with the old system and a decline in the power of kinship and clan. The old extended family concept had now given way to individualism--the power of the secret ballot cast by voters in their own name and not in the name of the lineage or clan.

The change in the Seneca political process met with the approval of the U. S. Federal Government, the State of New York, and by the tone of this notation in The Friend, also the Quakers of Philadelphia.

> The Seneca Nation of Indians--among the revolutionary movements in this age of progress, is the subversion of the ancient government of the Seneca Indians, which was an oligarchy in the hands of hereditary chiefs, and the substitution of elective headmen or council by the people of the tribe. The change was recognized by Congress at its last session, and has not received the sanction of the Legislature of this State, passed the House on Thursday, and the Senate yesterday. Albany Argus, April 7, (1849)[132]

The replacement of hereditary chiefs with elected ones did not by any means diminish the ardor of the traditionalists. Deposed chiefs and followers of Handsome Lake joined forces and there was a great revival of the old songs, dances and festivals. It was this kind of a reaction that Lewis H. Morgan saw when he journeyed from Rochester, New York to Cold Spring shortly after the great social and political upheavals. A very fortunate time for an anthropologist to arrive on the scene for a study of Seneca culture as it existed in the past.

> . . .the pagans gained strength as the parties on both reservations made common cause. Dances were multiplied, old ceremonies revived, and great effort was put forth to add interest and eclat to the proceedings. . .The influence of Christianity had been almost paralyzed by the intense excitement of the popular mind during the treaty struggle.[133]

The elective process brings with it groups of people who have recognized similarity of interests These groups coalesce and with that emerge political parties.

Peter Crouse, the old captive, had died in 1847 thereby just missing the great Seneca revolution in 1848. But before he died, Peter had taken an active interest in tribal affairs, and according to legend on the Allegany Reservation, was often sought out for advice. Some of this must have influenced his children as we find documentation that Peter T. Crouse, son of the captive became involved in the new politics.

Quaker records show that Peter T. Crouse had opened a school in 1837, discontinued it in 1841, then reopened it in 1842. Apparently still having time for politics, it was reported to the Quaker Committee that he joined the new Government Party and signed papers opposing treaties of sale of lands and emigration of the Senecas to the west[134]

With Seneca politics modified and operating more in the manner of white society with its political parties and voting, the two groups moved toward a more common ground. This could be seen in the spirit of cooperation between the Seneca and white society in the building of the Thomas Indian School. "Charter in hand, the trustees obtained a lot of fifteen acres, and after unavoid able hindrances, the cornerstone was laid on September 4, (1855) with 5,000 people in attendance.[135]

AUTHOR WITH SENECA ARTIFACTS: TURTLE RATTLE; FALSE FACE "BROKEN NOSE" MADE BY LESTER JIMERSON; AND BEADED NECKLACE MADE BY HAZEL THOMPSON.
PHOTO COURTESY MUHLENBERG COLLEGE RELATIONS DEPARTMENT

Fenton goes on to note that at the dedication of the Thomas School an old Indian responded to the speech of a state official that it was true that in the past the two races had tried to destroy each other but now they met for "mutual sympathies and deeds of kindness." It is also noted by Fenton that the tension between Christian and Pagan factions had relaxed.[136]

One can also see signs of this improved cooperation on the reservations such as the decision of the Senecas at Allegany to build their new community center next to the Longhouse at Steamburg, New York. This makes it possible to share a nicely paved parking lot, and locker room facilities at the center can be used by performers at the Longhouse or people who are attending the dances and functions.[137]

Relations with state governments had been strained in the turmoil and chaos of the frontier. Often homicides by whites or Indians caused rifts between the tribal councils and state representatives. Little Beard and three other chiefs, feeling the need to mend relationships after the murder of three Indians, sent a letter to the Governor of Pennsylvania urging him to "brighten the chain of friendship, as it is very rusty."[138]

Seneca relations with New York State were very good after the 1848 revolution. The state legislature had helped pave the way for political change when it passed the law of 1845. The state's action showed sympathy for the Seneca position and may have been suggestive as to possible remedies for the situation. When the new government of the Senecas came into power, the State of New York gave its recognition of it and directed state agents to act through the new government.[139]

By 1940, Seneca relations with the State of Pennsylvania had improved to the point where they decided to adopt Governor James into the Seneca Nation. He was given the name O-dahn-goht which means Sunlight in the Seneca language. The Senecas took it seriously and the Governor took it seriously enough to join in the dancing.[140]

Seneca relations with the Frederal government started very early. As part of the Iroquois Federation, the Senecas were involved in the Treaty of Fort Stanwix in 1784. This was the first treaty with the new United States Government and it was to leave the Iroquois with undisputed possession of Western New York State.[141]

After the political upheaval of the Senecas in 1848, the Federal Government recognized the Seneca Nation as the New York State government had done. The U. S. Government from 1848 on conducted its business with the Seneca Indians through the elected chiefs rather than hereditary chiefs.

The U. S. Federal Government maintains the rolls of recognized members of the Seneca nation and among other annuities and payments due them does not neglect the calico cloth disbursement.

> The U. S. Government made its 146th annual payment of six yards of calico today to each Indian of the Iroquois Confederacy in solemn accordance with the Treaty of Canandaigua.
> signed Nov. 11, 1794[142]

The political system of the Iroquois has undergone change over the years just as other aspects of their culture had to modify and adapt to the white man's presence. It may not be ideal and the traditionalists would undoubtedly prefer to have their system the way it used to be in the past but it has survived. Through their willingness to change, the Senecas have assured themselves of a future with their own distinct identity and strong ties to past tradition.

FOOTNOTES

CHAPTER 6

[1]Turner, loc. cit., p. 144.

[2]William Walton, 1740-1824 A Narrative of the Captivity of Benjamin Gilbert (Philadelphia: Cruckshank, 1784), p. 16.

[3]Current Anthropology, Vol. 4, 1963, p. 525.

[4]The Republican Press Salamanca, New York, 9/18/11.

[5]The Friend, Vol XX, 1847, p. 310.

[6]Ibid., p. 315.

[7]O'Reilly Papers, loc. cit. Vol. 8, Letters from Secretary of War Knox.

[8]American Philos. Soc., Vol. 97, 1953, p. 597.

[9]Pennsylvania History, Vol. XIX, 1952, p. 127.

[10]Jackson, loc. cit., p. 33.

[11]Lankes, loc. cit., p. 13.

[12]O'Reilly Papers, Vol. 13 (1798) Letter by John Pierce.

[13]Amer. Philos. Soc., loc. cit. p. 610.

[14]Boyd, loc. cit., p. 18.

[15]Ibid., p. 19.

[16]O'Reilly Papers, Vol. 10, Council at Buffalo Creek, Feb. 10, 1794.

[17]Snyderman, loc. cit., p. 617.

[18]Adams, loc. cit., p. 1107.

[19]Trippe, loc. cit., p. 3.

[20]Parker, loc. cit., p. 157.

[21]Alden, An account of, loc. cit., p. 12.

[22]Interview with Dema Crouse Stoffer, 1972.

[23]Trippe, loc. cit.

[24]The Friend, Vol XXI, 1847, p. 42. Sharpless

[25]Ibid., Vol. XXII, 1848, p. 342. Elkington

[26]Congdon, loc. cit., p. 122.

[27]Francello field notes 1972.

[28]Fenton, loc. cit., Ethnohistory 1957, p. 304.

[29]Turner, loc. cit., p. 222.

[30]Walker D. Wyman and Clifton B. Kroeber, Frontier in Perspective Madison: University of

Wisconsin Press, 1957), p. 231.

[31]*Current Anthropology* Vol. 4, 1963, p.525.

[32]Amer. Philos. Soc., *loc. cit.*, p. 574.

[33]*Western Penna. History Magazine* Vo. 24, 1941-42, p. 15.

[34]*Ibid.*, pp. 17-18.

[35]Snyderman, *loc. cit.*, p. 620.

[36]*Ibid.*

[37]*Pennsylvania History*, Vol. XIX, 1952, p. 128.

[38]*Ibid.*, p. 132.

[39]Draper Manuscript, *Diary of Henry Simmons, Jr.*, p. 4.

[40]*Ibid.*,

[41]Amer. Philos. Soc., *loc. cit.*, p. 567.

[42]*Ibid.*,

[43]Buffalo Historical Society, Vol. 6, 1903, p. 165.

[44]*Ibid.*, p. 166.

[45]William E. Strong, *The Story of the American Board* (Boston: The Pilgrim Press, 1910), pp. 41-42.

[46]*Ethnohistory*, Vol. 4, p. 318.

[47]*Ibid.*, p. 319.

[48]Tome, *loc. cit.*, p. 231.

[49]Amer. Philos. Soc., *loc. cit.*, p. 575.

[50]*Ibid.*

[51]*Ibid.*, p. 579.

[52]Caswell, *loc. cit.*, p. 53.

[53]*Ibid.*, pp. 57-58.

[54]Strong, *loc. cit.*, p. 186.

[55]Adams, *loc. cit.*, p. 40.

[56]Alden, *An account*, loc. cit., p. 12.

[57]Congdon, *loc. cit.*, p. 70.

[58]Trippe, *loc. cit.*, p. 6.

[59]*Ibid.*, p. 8.

[60]*Ibid.*, p. 9.

[61]*Ibid.*, p. 11.

[62]*Ibid.*, p. 13.

[63]Congdon, *loc. cit.*, p. 125.

[64]Buffalo Historical Society, Vol. 6, 1903, p. 166.

[65]*Ibid*., p. 267.

[66]Parkman, *loc*. *cit*., p. xlviii.

[67]Trippe, *loc*. *cit*., p. 13.

[68]Jackson, *loc*. *cit*., p. 49.

[69]Drake, *loc*. *cit*., p. 312.

[70]*Ibid*., p. 313.

[71]American Philos. Soc., *loc.* *cit*., p. 573.

[72]Turner, *loc*. *cit*., p. 510.

[73]Buffalo Historical Society, *loc*. *cit*., p. 267.

[74]Turner, *loc*. *cit*., p. 509.

[75]*The Friend*, Vol. XXII, p. 388.

[76]Congdon, *loc*. *cit*., p. 76.

[77]Amer. Philos. Soc., p. 575.

[78]*O'Reilly Papers*, loc. cit., Vol. 15, Personal Memoir of Thomas Morris.

[79]*Pennsylvania Archaeologist*, Vol. XVIII, 1948, p. 48.

[80]Wallace, Anthony, *loc*. *cit*., p. 205.

[81] The Friend, Vol. XXII, p. 342.

[82] Jackson, loc. cit., p. 10.

[83] Ibid.,

[84] Western Pennsylvania History Magazine, Vol. 24-25, p. 16.

[85] Diary of Henry Simmons, Jr., loc. cit., p. 27.

[86] Jackson, loc. cit., p. 34.

[87] Western Pennsylvania History Magazine, loc. cit., pp. 17-18.

[88] Ibid.,

[89] The Friend, Vol. XIX, 1846, p. 262.

[90] Jackson, loc. cit., p. 77.

[91] The Friend, Vol. XXII, 1849, p. 350.

[92] The Friend, Vol XXIII, 1851, p. 34.

[93] Ibid.

[94] Tome, loc. cit., p. 235.

[95] Ibid., pp. 233-234.

[96] Ibid.

[97] Alden, An Account, loc. cit., p. 12.

[98] *Ibid*., p. 30.

[99] *The Minutes and Papers of the Indian Committee 1837-1853* Vol. 3, (Philadelphia: Quaker Archives), p. 25.

[100] *Ibid*., p. 107.

[101] *Lyman C. Draper Manuscript Collection*, Series F, Vol. 16, Brant Papers, p. 234.

[102] *Seneca Nation Educational Foundation Fact Sheet*, Mr. Peterson, Director, 1977.

[103] *Draper Manuscript Collection*, Vol. 4S, p. 70.

[104] *Ibid*., pp. 70-71.

[105] *Western Pennsylvania History*, *loc*. *cit*., p. 16.

[106] *Ibid*., p. 17.

[107] *Pennsylvania History*, Vol. XIX, 1952, p. 343.

[108] O'Reilly Collection, *loc*. *cit*., Vol. 14, Letter of Chapin to Dearborn.

[109] *Bureau of American Ethnography Bulletin 156*, Smithsonian Institute, p. 6.

[110] Snyderman, *loc*. *cit*., p. 517.

[111] *Diary of H. Simmons, Jr*., *loc*. *cit*., p. 27

[112]*Ibid*., p. 16.

[113]*The Friend,* Vol. XX, 1847, p. 310.

[114]Amer. Philos. Soc., *loc*. *cit*., p. 573.

[115]*Ibid*., p. 574.

[116]Congdon, *loc*. *cit*., p. 66.

[117]*Diary of H. Simmons, Jr.*, *loc*. *cit*., p. 19

[118]*The Friend*, Vol. XXII, 1849, p. 342.

[119]*O'Reilly Papers*, *loc*. *cit*., Vol. 14.

[120]Amer. Philos.Soc., *loc*. *cit*., p. 574.

[121]Jackson, *loc*. *cit*., p. 43.

[122]*Ibid*., p. 41.

[123]Drake, *loc*. *cit*., p. 86.

[124]Snyderman, *loc*. *cit*., p. 617.

[125]Amer. Philos. Soc., *loc*. *cit*., p. 576

[126]*Ibid*., p. 574.

[127]Western Pennsylvania History, *loc*. *cit*., p. 20.

[128]*Ethnohistory*, *loc*. *cit*., p. 315.

[129]Amer. Philos. Soc., *loc*. *cit*., p. 575.

[130] *Ibid*., p. 577.

[131] Snyderman, *loc*. *cit*., p. 617.

[132] *The Friend*, Vol. XXII, 1849, p. 240.

[133] Amer. Philos. Soc., 1956, *loc*. *cit*., pp. 578-579.

[134] *Minutes and Papers of the Indian Committee loc. cit.*, p. 215.

[135] Amer. Philos. Soc., *loc*. *cit*., p. 580.

[136] *Ibid*., p. 581.

[137] Francello field notes 1974.

[138] *O'Reilly* Papers, 1948, Vol. 6.

[139] Amer. Philos. Soc., *loc*. *cit*., p. 578.

[140] *Pennsylvania Archaeologist*, Vol. X, 1940, p. 76.

[141] Adams, *loc*. *cit*., p. 29.

[142] *New York Times*, December 15, 1940.

CHAPTER 7

SENECA LEGACY

The great Chiefs and Sachems of the past are gone. Cornplanter, Farmer's Brother, Handsome Lake, Blacksnake, and the others have passed on to join their brothers in the world beyond our world. What kind of legacy did these great men leave for the generations of today?

The Seneca legacy of today is a great and powerful one. A strong and vigorous people with a dynamic culture has left its imprint on the generations that have come and those yet to come. The legacy has physical, cultural, spiritual, economic and political dimensions.

Most obvious of the physical is the people themselves. Despite war, disease, hunger and deprivations of the last two centuries, the people have survived! Not only survived but they also have regained their numbers so that today there are approximately six thousand Senecas throughout New York State and Canada.[1]

Land is another part of their physical legacy Somehow with the help of people such as Reverend Asher Wright, and Iroquoianists such as Lewis H. Morgan, and occasional evidence of concern on the part of the U. S. Federal Government and New York State, they were able to hold on to some acreage.

The Allegany Reservation land is a forty-two mile strip, one mile wide, with half a mile on each side of the Allegheny River from Vandalia, New York (just below the city of Olean) downriver to a point slightly below the New York State border and a short distance north of Warren, Pennsylvania.

The Cattaraugus Reservation north of the Allegheny Reservation is somewhat smaller, and follows a portion of Cattaraugus Creek to Lake Erie.

These two reservations are the legal property of the Seneca Nation of Indians which is an incorporated entity under New York State law pursuant to the Act of 1845.

Some of the physical legacy of the Allegany territory has been compromised by the building of the Kinzua Dam near Warren, Pa. The Seneca Nation lost its legal fight against the dam even though they took it all the way to the United States Supreme Court. The back-up waters from the dam flood approximately 9,000 of the best acreage on the Allegany Reservation. It put completely under water the Indian village at Cold Spring, including the old Longhouse there. Many Senecas had to be relocated, among them descendants of Peter Crouse, as the flood mark was set by the U. S. Army Corps of Engineers at 1,365 feet elevation.

Peter Crouse's homestead and lands are now under water. Sometimes if the water is low, the old road which went past his house may be seen within two hundred yeards of where he lived.[2]

The Seneca Nation was compensated for its loss by monetary payment and the building of new homes on higher ground for those whose residences were below the floodwater mark. Perhaps with some sense of humor, officials pointed out to the Indians that their land would not be under water all the time as the water level would subside during dry periods and they would be free to use it then! Meanwhile, the fishing is good in the lake.

In 1794 Chief Cornplanter had told the government Indian agent Chapin and some other government officials at Buffalo Creek: "We want room for our children,--It will be hard for them not to have country to live in after that we are gone."[3]

In 1965 Chief Cornplanter's descendants were fleeing the rising waters, leaving the site of the Cornplanter grant in Pennsylvania to find refuge on higher ground over the border into New York State. Even the Cornplanter monument, the first monument erected to an Indian in the United States had to be moved. The supposedly minority-conscious Warren Court had earlier sent word from Washington that Indians could have their property taken away from them in the twentieth century whether they agreed to it or not. They did receive some compensation this time, though.

Another part of the physical legacy is the material aspect of their culture. Indians still make a number of items, particularly in wood, which they use themselves or sell for added income Baskets are probably the most popular tourist item but they also make spoons, bowls, trays, ornaments and masks. These items are available in varying degrees of skill and authenticity.

And what of Peter Crouse; is there a physical legacy of his? Even though his old homestead and his former fields are under water, there is a physical legacy in the hundreds upon hundreds of descendants of the former captive. Peter's own large family and the large family of his second son, George W., ensured the presence of many Crouses in the years to follow. The "Crouse Association" of descendants of Peter Crouse is active to this day.

Reservation life today shows considerable carry-over of cultural attitudes and values from previous times. The Senecas don't live in longhouses anymore or even log cabins but the closeness of reservation society has a stamp of its own. Fenton, who has spent a great deal of time on the Seneca Reservation, has written sensitively on this point.

> I have also felt the warmth of Reservation society, the slackening of tensions as one settles into reservation life, its 'come eat with us' hospitality, the loyalty of kin and sibling, the sense of having a name and identification with a clan, and even being married into another

> clan. No one ever interrupts anyone else and whoever speaks is heard to the end.[4]

The long periods of hostility that engulfed the Senecas in the seventeenth and eighteenth centuries have put a warlike stamp on their culture. This fills the pages of the white man's "American History." It is very easy to overlook the peaceful side of the Senecas and other Iroquois people. There is a tendency on the part of whites to pass over the cultural values of the Senecas which placed a high value on getting along well with others and the avoidance of personal animosities. The Senecas at home, Parker points out, were kind considerate, hospitable, and genial.[5] He writes that the real source of power was not their political organization but "the dynamic ideals and moral force of its social organization."[6]

This strong force may be seen on the Reservation today. The preservation of their cultural symbols in addition to this moral force give the present-day Senecas a rich heritage from which to draw. Some will choose one part, some another, resulting in a variety of cultural expressions in Seneca behavior today.

> Apart from individual variations in behavior which arise at psychological levels. . .I noted first among the Seneca diversity of individual expression which struck me as being the product of the peculiar participation. . . individuals participate differently in affairs which are their common social heritage.[7]

The cultural legacy of the Indian has also become a part of the legacy of white America. Although it is well known that the Indian borrowed from white society, it is not so generally known that white society also borrowed from them. Professor Hallowell has written on the impact of the of the Indian on American culture.

> . . .the Indian had a deep influence on our speech, our economic life, our clothing, our sports and recreations, certain indigenous religious cults, many of our curative practices, folk and concern music, the novel, poetry, drama, even some of our basic psychological attitudes, and one of the social sciences, anthropology.[8]

The Senecas alone did not do all these things for American society but they were part of the overall North American Indian culture to which Hallowell is making reference, They contributed their share and in keeping with Seneca cultural values, it was a generous share.

A religious people by long tradition, the spiritual life of the Senecas today remains strong rich, and colorful. Not only are there traditionalists and Christians but also those who participate in both. Upon enquiring of an Indian how he could be a Christian and also take part in the other religious ceremonies, I was told that Seneca warriors and hunters always took two bowstrings with them on the trail. If one didn't work, then maybe the other would.[9]

Actually, the two religious views are not absolutely exclusive. The basis of their traditional religion is thanksgiving to the Creator for the things the Senecas receive through nature to use and cherish, a concept not alien to Christianity. The missionary, Reverend Asher Wright, saw the "present system of paganism" as he called it, borrowing heavily from Jesuit teachings.

> Our present pagan population regard the White man's religion as never intended for the Indians, still notwithstanding retain the rosary in the belt of wampum and the mass for the dead under the name

> of the funeral feast; the notion of purgatory in the temporary punishment in hell for various sorts of sins, and Confessional in their yearly assemblies, where the penitent recites his sins, fingering over the strings of wampum, and promises amendment.[10]

The good Quaker Halliday Jackson had to admit that in telling his followers that they should not drink whiskey, Handsome Lake was on the same track as the Quakers. What Jackson was displeased about was the collective aspects of the Prophet's preaching in which he told his followers not to sell anything which they raised on their land, but give it away to one another, and especially to their old people.[11] Although Jackson did not like this because it appeared to him to be connected with their old way, it could be interpreted by others as good Christian charity.

In writing about the Cornplanter group of Seneca Indians, Deardorff noted that though Christians, with increased age the old spirits beckoned them more strongly.

> The Cornplanters have been church members for years, but they have not lost all interest in the council house and what goes on there. Especially as they get older the festivals draw them; Strawberry in the spring, Green Corn in the fall, and New Year's at the right January moon, with the Husk faces on the fifth night.[12]

The economic legacy is a much-improved one over the terrible years of the late eighteenth century and the first half of the nineteenth. It is much more complicated than that of the French, Dutch, and English trading days but it is bringing some rewards of economic significance to the Seneca.

To begin with, the Treasury of the Seneca

Nation is amply filled. Various monies have come in, ranging from federal annuities to mineral royalties for sand, gravel, and natural gas. Because the title to the Reservation is vested in severalty to the Seneca Nation, individuals who hold property have only surface rights to the land. Anything underneath belongs to all the nation and proceeds go to the Nation's Treasury.

Since U. S. Federal law forbids the sale of reservation land to non-Indians, land holders are always Indians although they may lease land for short periods of time. When a landholder dies, the land can be inherited only by individuals who are certified to be Senecas, appearing on the federal rolls as such. A person cannot be on these rolls if his or her mother was not a Seneca. This is in keeping with the U.S. Government decision to abide by the matrilineal tradition of the Senecas. The female dominance so codified gives the Seneca female a decided advantage as she can choose either a reservation male or non-reservation non-Indian male and her children will still qualify to be on the rolls. The Seneca male must choose a Seneca female if he wishes to have his children on the rolls and qualified to inherit his property.[13]

The greatest threat to the reservation system is the taking of land by outside people. Some land has been lost through highway acquisition by the State of New York. There is compensation for this to the Seneca Nation and the state assumes jurisdiction of all state roads.

Land lost as a result of the building of the Kinzua Dam was compensated for in payment to the Nation and in some cases in land trade off with a nearby state park. The Kinzua settlement was unusual in that a trust fund for educational purposes was set up to compensate for loss to future generations. This fund is invested and is millions of dollars in value.

Another threat to the reservation system is

the process of "termination" which would phase out all federal and state controls over the Indians as a specific group. This act, passed during the Eisenhower Administration, seeks to bring to an end the special relationship between the government and the Indian. It would mean the lifting of the ban on sale of reservation property and, like the Dawes Act in the latter part of the nineteenth century, could probably see the Indian acreage shrink disastrously. With changes in administrations in Washington, the termination concept has been put in abeyance. Economically, the termination proposal was greatly feared because in addition to the probably dissolvement of Indian lands, there was the specter of local, state, and federal taxation. The reservation is not only a rallying place for cultural heritage, it is also a tax shelter.

Educational costs for Seneca children are now borne by the State of New York. Gone are the one-room schools that dotted the Reservation in preious years. Yellow buses take the Senecas' children, the same as they do other children, to central learning centers in the various nearby districts. In the new Seneca School in Salamanca, a descendant of Peter Crouse carries on the tradition set by the captive's son, Peter T. Crouse, as a teacher of Seneca schoolchildren.

For these Seneca young men and women who wish to go to post-secondary school, there is a generous amount of financial aid. The Seneca Nation Education Foundation provides scholarships, as does the State of New York, and also the Federal Government. No youngster need drop out of college or fear going to college because of cost. In 1972 seventy per cent of Seneca students who were graduated from high school went on to further study. A total of 132 students attending colleges or technical schools received approximately $110,880 in scholarships paid for that year.[14]

Students graduated from colleges or technical schools in recent years have been in the following fields:

- Art Education
- English
- Liberal Arts
- Sociology
- Business Administration
- Law
- Secretarial Science
- Medical Secretary
- Drafting
- Chef
- Computer Programming
- Beauty Culture
- Nursing
- Fine Arts
- Music

Employment off the Reservation gives the Senecas a chance to bring in some funds to supplement their reservation resources. They hold a variety of jobs in white society and usually prefer to return to the Reservation when their work allows. It is a much more relaxed atmosphere and it gives a person a chance to visit with friends and neighbors. Speaking of the Cornplanter group but probably equally applicable to all Senecas, Deardorff comments:

> Most of the Cornplanter heirs are out and about, hustling for livings as teachers, preachers, lawyers, railroad men, artisans, and farmers. But here on the Grant there is no place for these things. One should keep fat and warm and well with as little work as possible so that he may have time to live.[15]

Recently the Senecas received checks in the mail from a repentant Uncle Sam. These checks or "settlement money" are an attempt to repay the Senecas for land that was illegally taken from them over a century ago when the land companies voraciously devoured millions of acres belonging to their people. The U.S.Government gave the Senecas the option of receiving the money as a group in which case it would have gone to the Nation's Treasury, or receiving the money individually. The vote was in favor of the latter and home coffers benefitted.

The economy looks good for the Senecas, not too much need to worry. As Deardorff put it:

> Life on the Grant (and the Reservation, too) goes on at an easy gait. . .cellars are full of dried corn and squash; canned dandelion, wild onion, fruits, and berries; and jars of venison and noodles. There is plenty of wood and no one is cold.[16]

The political legacy of the Senecas is a rich and strong one as befitting a people with centuries of tradition in the arts of persuasion, negotiation, and agreement. Seneca political development was unusually complex for a people in the horticultural-hunter-gatherer stage of technology and economics.

When the colonies were casting about for a way to organize their disparate interests, Benjamin Franklin first suggested the Albany plan and then later was a guiding light at the Constitutional Convention in Philadelphia.

> It has ever been said that information about the organizations and operation of the League of the Iroquois, which Franklin picked up at various Indian Councils, suggested to him the pattern for a United States of America. . .[17]

On the reservations at Allegany and Cattaraugus today, the political legacy is evident in the very active politics that takes place in the affairs of the Seneca Nation. Similar to the United States political structure, there are two major parties but they are not Republicans and Democrats. They have their own traditions in the People's Party and the New Deal party. The election pot boils in November for reservation politics just as it does anywhere else in the United States.

The old love of politics is still there and new orators have risen to take the place of the old. Affairs of the Seneca Nation are looked after in a new stone building on the Allegany Reservation, having the office space, personnel, and administrative officials that any modern municipality would have in New York State.

The Seneca Nation today is strong and vigorous. A great peope has demonstrated that it can meet incredible adversity and survive the ordeal with renewed strength and wisdom. A centuries-old culture can look confidently to the future, secure in the knowledge that it can meet new problems and dangers with old wisdom and everpresent vitality.

And what of old Peter, the white captive? Did he make a wise coice when he rejected the white man's society for that of his red brothers in the forest? The long and fruitful life of Peter Crouse is convincing evidence that the captive made a wise choice. His many descendants have had an important influence on the life of the Seneca Nation and are living testimony to the wisdom of his choice. The benefits received by the Senecas from the contributions of hundreds upon hundreds of Crouse descendants are valuable dividends for a great and deserving people.

Daw-nayhoh!
It is done!

FOOTNOTES

CHAPTER 7

[1]Estimate by former President of the Seneca Nation Leo C. Cooper. Some members of the nation live off the Reservation but are affiliated and identify culturally with it.

[2]Seneca informant Leo C. Cooper.

[3]O'Reilly Papers, loc. cit., Vol. 10.

[4]Amer. Philos. Soc., loc. cit., p. 581.

[5]Parker, loc. cit., p. 151.

[6]Ibid., pp. 50-51.

[7]William N. Fenton, The Iroquois Eagle Dance, an Offshoot of the Calumet Dance. Smithsonian Institution Bureau of American Ethnology Bulletin 156. (Washington: U.S. Government Printing Office, 1953), pp. 8-9.

[8]Wyman and Kroeber, loc. cit., p. 229.

[9]Seneca Informant Leo C. Cooper

[10]Ethnohistory, 1957, Vol. 4, pp. 3-5.

[11]Jackson, loc. cit., p. 43.

[12]Western Pennsylvania History, loc. cit., p. 20.

[13]There is some speculation as to how the federal laws banning discrimination on the basis

of sex might apply here. Passage of equal rights amendment to U.S. Constitution would increase that speculation.

[14] Seneca Nation Education Foundation Fact Sheet

[15] Western Pennsylvania History, loc. cit., p. 20.

[16] Ibid.

[17] Wyman and Kroeber, loc. cit., p. 232.

BIBLIOGRAPHY

Adams, William. Historical Gazetteer and Biographical Memorial of Cattaraugus County, New York. Syracuse: Lyman, Horton & Co., 1893.

Alden, Timothy. An Account of Sundry Missions Performed Among the Senecas and Munsees. 1771-1839. New York: J. Seymour, 1827.

__________, The Alleghany Magazine (or) Repository of Useful Knowledge. Vol. I, No. I Meadville, Pa.: Thomas Atkinson III July MDCCCXVI.

Aldrich, Charles. "Recollections of the Senecas," Annals of Iowa, Series 3, Vol. VII, April January 1905-7. Des Moines.

Beauchamp, William M. The Life of Conrad Weiser. Syracuse: Onondaga Historical Association, 1925.

Boyd, Thomas. Simon Girty the White Savage. New York: Minton, Balch & Co., 1928.

Caswell, Harriet S. Our Life Among the Iroquois Indians. Boston: Congregational Sunday School and Publishing Society, 1892.

Congdon, Charles Edwin. Allegany Oxbow. Little Valley, New York: Straight Publishing Co.,

Deardorff, Merle H. Collection. Harrisburg: Pennsylvania Archives.

__________, Diary of Henry Simmons, Jr. 1796-1800. (microfilm) Pennsylvania Historical and Museum Commission.

Drake, Samuel G. Indian Biography, Boston: Josiah Drake, 1832.

Fenton, William N. "Toward the Gradual Civilization of the Indian Natives," Proceedings of the American Philosophical Society, Vol. 100, No. 6, December 1956.

________, The Iroquois Eagle Dance, an Offshoot of the Calumet Dance. Smithsonian Institution Bureau of American Ethnology Bulletin 156. Washington: U.S.Government Printing Office, 1953.

________, Unpublished Genealogy of Peter Crouse Descendants. 1933 Field Work.

________, (ed.) "Seneca Indians by Asher Wright" (1859). Ethnohistory. Vol. 4, 1957.

Hallowell, A. Irving. "American Indians, White and Black: the Phenomenon of Transculturalization," Current Anthropology, Vol. 4. No. 5.

Heckewelder, John. History, Manners, and Customs of the Indian Nations. Vol XII. Historical Society of Pennsylvania, 1876.

Hulbert, Archer B. and Schwarze, William N. David Zeiberger's History of the Northern American Indians. Ohio State Archaeological and Historical Society, 1910.

Jackson, Halliday. Civilization of the Indian Natives. Philadelphia: Gould, 1830.

Kent, Donald H. and Deardorff, Merle H. "John Adlum on the Allegheny," Pennsylvania Magazine of History and Biography, Vol. 84, 1960.

LaFarge, Oliver. A Pictorial History of the American Indian. New York: Crown Publishers, Inc., 1956.

Lankes, Frank J. The Senecas on Buffalo Creek Reservation. West Seneca, N. Y.: West Seneca Historical Society, 1964.

Maclay, Samuel. Journal 1790. Williamsport, Pa.: John F. Meginness, 1887.

Merrifield, Edward. The Story of the Captivity and Rescue from the Indians of Luke Swetland. Scranton, Pa., 1915.

Morgan, Lewis H. League of the Iroquois. Secaucus, N. J.: The Citadel Press, 1972.

O'Reilly, Henry. Papers Pertaining to the Six Nations. Selections from Vols. 6-15. Owned and filmed by New York Historical Society, 1948.

Parker, Arthur C. The History of the Seneca Indians. Empire State Historical Publication XLIII. Port Washington, N. Y.: Ira J. Friedman, Inc., 1967.

Parkman, Francis. The Jesuits in North America. 8th Edition. Boston: Little, Brown & Co., 1874.

Rupp, I. Daniel. Early History of Western Pennsylvania and of the West. Pittsburgh, Pa.: Daniel W. Kauffman, 1846.

Severance, Frank H. "Quakers Among the Senecas," Buffalo Historical Society, Vol. 6, 1903, Buffalo: Buffalo Historical Society.

Smith, Robert (ed.). "The Friend" Vol. XVIII Philadelphia: Joseph Kite and Co., 1845.

__________, Vols. 1-24, 1838-1850, Ann Arbor: Michigan University Microfilm.

Snyderman, George S. Behind the Tree of Peace. Ph. D. Dissertation, Philadelphia, Pa.: University of Pennsylvania, 1948.

_______, (ed.) The Manuscript Collections of the

Philadelphia Yearly Meeting of Friends Pertaining to the American Indian. Arch Street Philadelphia, Pa.

Stern, Bernhard J. (ed.) "The Letters of Asher Wright to Lewis Henry Morgan," American Anthropologist, Vol. 35, 1933.

Strong, William E. The Story of the American Board. Boston: The Pilgrim Press, 1910.

Thwaites, Reuben G. and Kellogg, Louise P. The Revolution on the Upper Ohio, 1775-1777. Madison: Wisconsin Historical Society, 1908

Tome, Philip. Pioneer Life or Thirty Years a Hunter. Arno Press, 1971.

Turner, O. Pioneer History of the Holland Purchase Buffalo: Jewett, Thomas & Co., 1849.

Wallace, Anthony F. C. The Death and Rebirth of the Seneca. New York: Alfred A. Knopf, 1970

________, (ed.) Halliday Jackson's Journal to the Seneca Indians, 1798-1800. Pennsylvania History, Vol XIX, 1952.

Wallace, Paul A. W. Indians in Pennsylvania. Harrisburg, Pa.: Historical and Museum Commission, 1975.

Walton, William. 1740-1824 A Narrative of the Captivity of Benjamin Gilbert. Philadelphia: Crukshank, 1784.

Wyman, Walker D. and Kroeber, Clifton B. (eds.) The Frontier in Perspective. Madison: University of Wisconsin Press, 1957.

PERIODICALS

American Anthropologist, Vol. 35, 1933.
Pennsylvania Archaeologist. Vol. X, No. 4, Oct.'40

________. Vol. XVI, No. 1, Jan. 1946.
Vol. XVIII, No. 3and 4, Fall '48

Western Pennsylvania Historical Magazine. Vols. 24-25, 1941-1942.

NEWSPAPER

The Republican Press. Salamanca, New York. Tuesday September 12, 1911.

MANUSCRIPTS

Draper, Lyman C. Manuscript Collection Daniel Brodhead Papers. Series H, Vol. 1-3, Madison: Historical Society of Wisconsin.

________, Series F, Vol. 16-18, Madison: Historical Society of Wisconsin.

________, Series S, Vol. 1-9, Madison: Historical Society of Wisconsin.

Trippe, M. F. Mrs. "Historical Facts Concerning Peter Crouse the Captive, His Wife Rachel, their Descendants and Their Times," William N. Fenton Holdings.

HISTORICAL PAPERS

American Philosophical Society, Proceedings of. Vol. 97, Philadelphia, 1953.

Elko, Town of. Folder of Historical Papers. Little Valley, N. Y.: Little Valley Historical Society, seen in 1974.

First Census of the United States 1790. Vol. 7, New York. Washington: Government Printing Office 1908.

Minutes and Papers of the Indian Committee, 1795-1815. Arch St., Philadelphia, Pa.:Quaker Archives.

Seneca Nation Educational Foundation Fact Sheet, 1972. Salamanca, New York.

Warren County, Pennsylvania Historical Society Volume, "Cornplanter Grant" and "Seneca Grant" Peter Crouse Section August 1927-June 1928.

INDEX